REAPER

Briana Robertson

Edited by
Katelyn Murphy, Lance Fling,
Donelle Pardee Whiting

1

REAPER

ISBN-13: 978-1-945263-24-8

DEDICATION

To my husband,3 Chaz, who else could I possibly dedicate my first officially published solitary work to? I love you, baby.

ACKNOWLEDGMENTS

—To Stitched Smile Publications, for taking a chance on me and my own personal take on horror.

—To Lisa Vasquez, quite simply the best CEO and mentor an emerging author could ask for; no one else does so much for her people.

—To Jeff Brown; there are no adequate words, sir, to say thank you for all you've done in making this dream a reality.

—To Donelle Pardee Whiting and Katelyn Murphy, for all your editing expertise; all the gratitude in the world for making my work shine.

—To my husband, Chaz, for everything.

—And finally, to my readers; I sincerely hope you enjoy … and maybe cry, just a little.

Table of Contents

REAPER

"Full house."

"Dammit, Thana! Fuck you."

I grin at my twin as she tosses her hand onto the table and folds her arms across her chest. Reaching over, I drag the pile of assorted bills and coins toward me and dig through it.

"Is this a Roman Denarius?" I hold the coin up to the light and squint, trying unsuccessfully to make out the illegible script.

"I don't know. Probably."

"Sweet!"6

That's the best part of beating Karen at cards; I never know what gems I'm going to find in the pool. She's always tossing in random and rare bits of money—a bronze obol here, a Willow Tree Threepence there—whatever happens to be in her pockets, or if we're playing for higher stakes, the multitude of glass jars hanging around the place. She's got quite the collection; then again, I guess that's what happens when your twin's been ferrying the dead around since nearly the beginning of time.

The thought puts a damper on my enthusiasm, and I lay the ancient Roman coin back on the table. I'm always gone by the time they give Karen their coin, so I have no idea who gave her this Denarius. But whoever it was, I was there; at some point in this interminable existence of mine, I met them, took their soul by the hand, and led them away from life.

"Hey. You okay?"

I look up to see Karen studying me and give myself a mental shake. "Yeah. Fine."

She cocks her head, her lips pursed; it's a look I'm familiar with, and it says quite succinctly: bullshit.

"You know I'm here for you, right?"

"Of course I do. Why would you say that?"

"Because I wonder sometimes. You can be so ..."

Depressing. Bereft. Cut off.

She doesn't say any of that, but I hear it nonetheless.

"I just ... I hate this, Karen. Sometimes I hate it so much I can barely breathe. And the fact that you're stuck in this with me, that I did this to you—"

"Thana. Thana, stop. Do you hear me? Stop. You didn't do this to me. We got dealt a lousy hand, that's all. But we're sisters, and I will always have your back. You got that? No matter what happens. No matter how bad shit gets. We're in this together; we always have been, and we always will be. So please, stop. This isn't your fault."

Except it is, Karen. It is.

Above our heads, an alarm sounds, cutting off the discussion. We both glance up, then at each other. Mirror images, our shoulders hunch, and we release twin huffs of breath.

Break's over.

It's been a whopping seven and a half minutes.

Rising to my feet, I follow her into her bedroom. She disappears into the closet; Seconds later, I reappear on my front porch, a billowing black cloak is hurled at my face. Catching it, I give it a hard shake, then whip it over my shoulders. By the time I've adjusted the clasp and raised the hood, Karen has emerged, also enshrouded in black. She holds out a six-foot scythe, the curved blade easily measuring a yard. Without hesitation, I grab it and settle it against my shoulder. It's a backup—my Jimmy Garappolo, so to speak—but it'll work. It has to, as Brady's safely ensconced in the closet at my place. I could go get him—it wouldn't take that long—but there's a reason Karen and I keep spares; it saves time.

In sync, we turn and head for the front door. Stepping outside, the sunlight glints off the freshly washed windows of Karen's rustic cabin. Corey must have been here recently; I don't know what sort of cleaner he uses, but somehow the glass glistens longer than any glass should. I should ask him about it someday. But then again, when would I have the time?

The sun beats down as I embrace my twin. Anyone else would be sweltering beneath the heavy, ebony robe, but I'm not. There's a reason people shiver when they think about death; I'm enveloped by an innate chill, and there's no escaping it whenever I venture near.

"I'll be back soon."

"I'll be waiting."

Before she can turn away, I call out.

"I love you, Karen."

"I know."

She shoots me a wink, and I can't help but grin. The exchange has been a favorite of ours ever since we sat in the Skyview Drive-In in 1980 and watched *The Empire Strikes Back*. She heads around the side of the cabin and down the embankment to the river's edge. With deft movements, she flips the sturdy, green canoe and slides it gently into the water. It drifts as far as the tied-off rope allows, then bounces back toward the dock.

Taking a deep breath, I focus and let myself dissipate into a swirling black mist. Moments later, I settle back into form just inside the sliding glass door of an ICU room.

Mitchell Hugh Donovan lies unconscious in the single hospital bed. His wife, Kismet, sits beside him, gently clasping his limp fingers, while a nurse moves slowly but surely around them, pulling out tubes and unhooking machines.

Kismet's eyes are bloodshot, and her cheeks are puffy. The skin beneath her nostrils is raw. Active grief has passed, leaving behind a passive numbness.

The scene is all too familiar.

The nurse exits the room, giving her arms an absent rub as she walks past me. She'll chalk it up to a draft, I'm sure. The doctor, who up until this point has remained silent and unobtrusive in a corner, steps forward, and my heart

8

twists as I listen to him give Kismet the company line.

"Mrs. Donovan, I'm so sorry for your loss."

The words sound as lifeless as Mitchell Donovan's about to be. Can she hear it? Or is it only me, because I have heard them so many times—I wouldn't even try to guess at how many.

People think they can empathize with the loss of a loved one, because everyone has lost someone. What no one ever seems to understand, is everyone loves differently. Everyone feels differently. And don't get me started on the countless ways someone can grieve.

The fact is, no one can truly understand someone else's loss.

No one … except me.

The force of Kismet's despair is a brutal wind that pummels me and nearly knocks me off my feet. My lungs burn as I drag a deep breath in and fight to keep my balance.

"Please, Doctor. I'd like to be alone."

The calm in her voice is a lie. She is reeling inside.

"I understand. The nurses will notify me when … when he …"

She nods in understanding and doesn't bother to look up as he too, exits the room. Once he's gone, I move closer, unseen.

Her arms are bandaged, hiding a severe case of road-rash. Her left lower leg is encased in a stark, white cast. A fairly deep, yet superficial, cut runs the length of her forehead and disappears into her hairline.

The scene before me shifts, and I'm speeding alongside a motorcycle. Mitch's hands rest loosely on the handlebars. Kismet rides behind him, her arms wrapped around his waist. The Mississippi River stretches out on our left, and to our right is the sheer face of a cliff. Mitch yells something over his shoulder—I can't make it out over the roar of the wind—and the two of them laugh.

We swing around a curve. A horn blares, followed by the screeching of tires and rending screams of tearing metal. Kismet is tossed off the side of the bike. She hits the pavement, skids and rolls. Mitch propels forward into the grill of a pick-up.

"Dammit, Mitch."

The memory dissolves. I'm back in the ICU room, watching Kismet watch Mitch as the last vestiges of life drain away from him.

"This isn't how things were supposed to happen. This isn't how our life is supposed to go. We've got so much left to do, together."

Her eyes well up with tears, and I feel my own prick. It seems silly, I know. For the gods' sake, I've been escorting the dead for eons. I should be used to this by now.

"You're here for me, aren't you?"

The ghostly essence of Mitchell Donovan floats a few feet away. I stare at him from beneath my hood and nod, my heart heavy with regret.

"I am. I'm sorry."

"You don't have to be. My mother's been warning me about that damn bike since I was sixteen. I just … I didn't think …" He looks back toward Kismet, who's still holding his hand and whispering to him, unaware his body's nothing more than an empty husk. He takes a shaky breath, and his voice quivers. "I don't want her to be alone."

"She won't be." The words are out before I can stop them.

The wispy smoke that is Mitch's face flashes back to me. "She'll find someone else, then?" The devastating mixture of hope and despair in his voice makes my stomach roil. He loves her so much; the idea that she'll love another after him is both his salvation and his damnation, and he can't decide which is worse.

I know *exactly* how he feels.

"No. She'll never take another lover."

"But … You said she wouldn't be alone. How …?"

Knowing I shouldn't, but unable to stop myself, I give a quick wave of my hand, and the scene dissolves. The hospital walls fade away, the bed disappears. We're standing in Mitch's living room. A fire crackles cheerfully in the grate, Christmas lights twinkle and glint in the windows and on a

six-foot tree, and Kismet sits cross-legged on the floor. A few feet away, a boy of about five giggles excitedly as he rips Frosty paper off a box nearly as big as he is. Inside is a Fisher-Price tool bench with a full set of tools.

With a whoop, he races into his mother's arms. "Santa brought it, Mommy! He brought it! He's the best, isn't he, Mommy? I can't believe it!"

Kismet laughs and hugs him tight. "He is the best. Merry Christmas, Mitch. I love you."

"I love you, too. Can we open it tonight, Mommy? Can we? Pretty please?"

With another wave, the colors of the scene wash away and seep back into the lifeless ICU room.

"We … We have a son?" Mitch stares at Kismet, who sits with an instinctual and unknowing hand on her belly.

"Yes."

"She's pregnant?"

"She is."

"Now?"

I nod.

"How long?"

"About six weeks. She won't realize she's missed her period for about another month."

"Wow …" Mitch raises a hand to wipe at his eyes. The tears aren't corporeal, but the action is inherent. "Dammit."

My heart wrenches at the regret and agony seeping from him. It's difficult, but somehow I hold my tongue and remain silent, giving him a final moment to grieve.

"It's not fair! It's too soon."

It always is.

"The driver of that damn truck should be in that fucking bed! I don't know what that asshole was doing—drinking, sleeping, on a fucking phone—but he came around that curve in the wrong damn lane. I've *always* been careful on my bike, and I never would have taken Kismet out if I thought ..."

He drifts off, shaking with repressed fury and palpable sorrow. "And now my son will grow up without a father. Because of a fucking dumbass driver. Dammit!"

The shout should echo, but sound doesn't exist in the vacuum of our presence. My heart is breaking for him, for his wife, and his unborn child. A thought crosses my mind, and I fight to stamp it out.

I can't. It's against the rules.

Perhaps it's the undying love shining in Kismet's tears. Or maybe it's an innate need to see justice served. Hell, most likely it's because I've been doing this for too damn long, and I just can't deal with it anymore. Whatever the reason, I let go of the invisible grip I hold on Mitchell Donovan.

His essence glows, and he is drawn slowly back toward the prostrate figure in the hospital bed. He looks up at me, his eyes wide.

"Wha … What's happening?"

"Go back to your family, Mitchell."

"But I thought … How?"

I just shake my head. "Take your life back. Love your wife. Witness the birth of your son. Live."

His eyes shimmer. "Thank you." The words are little more than a soundless whisper.

"Until we meet again, Mitchell Donovan."

The silvery mist congeals into a form resembling a man and is sucked into the body that once again holds Mitch's being. Suddenly, he bows off the bed, and with a wheeze, begins to cough uncontrollably.

Kismet shoots out of her chair and leans over him, her

hand on his chest.

"Mitch? Mitch!" She looks up and screams. "Nurse! Doctor!"

As members of the hospital staff rush in, I take my leave, drifting into naught but ether, and head for Karen's cabin.

She's standing in the doorway when I arrive. With long strides, she meets me halfway across the lawn, her eyes flashing.

"What the hell happened, Thana? What did you do?"

"What do you mean?"

Karen just stares at me with pursed lips and hands on hips. "Seriously? You're going to play dumb? Zenos is here, you idiot!"

My heart sinks. *Zenos*. Damn him. Damn him to hell and back, a million times over! Somehow, I force my shoulders to lift in a careless shrug.

"So what?"

"So what?!"

"What's he going to do, Karen? There's nothing worse he can do to me than what he's already done."

"He could kill you, Thana!"

"He won't."

I skirt around her and head for the front door, leaving her to stare, open-mouthed, after me. Stepping over the threshold, I pull the hood of my cloak back and set the scythe against the wall. I barely have a moment to brace myself before Zenos whirls toward me. Flames burn in his eyes, and his nostrils are flared wide. His hands are clamped tightly into fists; I can't help wondering if he's imagining my neck between them.

He is beyond furious.

"What the *fuck* do you think you're doing?" He roars the words; the force behind them is a cyclone that whips around the room, scattering the deck of cards and sending them flying. One of them catches the corner of my eye as it belts by, drawing a delicate stream of blood that heals almost instant-ly. I flinch, but just barely.

His rage is awesome, it's true, but what I told Karen is also true: he can't hurt me. Not anymore. So, not only do I stand my ground, I meet him toe-to-toe.

"Zenos. Always a pleasure to have you drop in. What brings you by?"

"Don't play innocent with me, Thana. You were sent to collect a soul."

"I know what I was sent to do, thank you. I've been doing it for a long while now, if you recall. Nearly forever."

"And yet, you return without Mitchell Donovan."

"Yes." I step around him and head for the open kitchen area. I need caffeine.

Zenos follows me. "Why, Thana?"

I shrug. "It wasn't his time."

A hand stronger than any hand has the right to be grips my bicep and tosses me around. I can't help it—I wince; my arm will bear the bruise for weeks. Such is the price for anger-ing the boss-man.

"What do you mean 'it wasn't his time?' That's not for you to say, Thana; *you* do not have the right to make such a choice. Now get back to that damn hospital and get him!"

"No!" I yank my arm away, not caring about the pain, and thrust my face close to his. He may tower over me, but I make a valiant effort. "Who has the right, if not me? You? Don? Karen? You're not there! You don't see them! You don't have to feel what they feel, what their loved ones feel. Hell, I doubt you even could, you heartless sonofabitch."

"Watch it, Thana. You're on shaky enough ground as it is."

"Fuck you, Zenos."

The slap takes me off guard, knocking me to the floor. My cheek literally burns from his fury; I raise trembling fingers to my face and press the flame out. They come away covered

14

in ash.

I don't bother to try and stop the laughter that bubbles from deep within my chest.

Zenos stares at me, eyes wide with incredulity.

"Is that the best you can do?" I rise to my feet and go back to assembling the necessities for a cup of coffee. "You really know how to ingratiate yourself on a girl, don't you, Zenos? Except … Wait a minute. Oh, that's right." I snap my fingers, turn to point one at him. "That's never really been your strong suit, has it?"

He's quivering with fury; the flames in his eyes are now joined by flashes of lightning. It's a telltale sign — one that lets me know I'm walking an extremely fine line. I should probably shut up now. Shut up, take my punishment — there's bound to be one — like a docile little Reaper, and let him go. But watching Mitchell and Kismet Donovan has kindled a fragile fire within me, and I'll be damned if I let him kick it out.

"How's Hadrian?" His quiet question is a well-aimed dagger to my heart, and he knows it. I'm surprised, though; usually it takes him a while to get to this point. My actions, followed by my own piercing comment, must really be pushing his buttons.

"You'd have to ask Karen. She sees him more often than I do."

"And how often is that?" His tone drips with snide sarcasm, a poisoned bite that sinks into me and spreads. Lifting the steaming coffee to my lips, I turn and face him.

"Never. I *never* see him, Zenos. You made damn sure of that, not that it's done you any good."

"It brings me immeasurable joy every time I think of it."

"Knowing you, I'm sure that's true. It almost makes me feel sorry for you."

He snorts at that and cocks a hip. "Sorry for me? How quaint."

I shake my head and turn away, sipping the brew and letting it burn on its way down.

"I have everything, Thana. I *am* everything. Everything on, above, and below the Earth is mine to control. How could you possibly feel sorry for me?"

I set the cup down, brace myself on the counter, and let my head dip. He still doesn't understand. He never has, and he never will. The point's not worth arguing, I know.

"C'mon. Tell me. You feel sorry for me, I want to know why."

Don't answer him, Thana. Just let it go. He'll leave soon enough. Don't give him a reason to stay.

His hands settle on my shoulders. In a flurry, he whirls me around to face him. "C'mon, Thana. Answer me."

Still I remain silent.

Furious, he shakes me. "I command you to answer me!"

My hand flies before I can stop it, my palm connecting soundly with his face. The resounding slap echoes in the small room, followed by a heavy silence that brims with his fiery jealousy and my bitter resentment.

"You arrogant, superior prick! How dare you? '*Command me?*' Are you fucking kidding me? You may technically be the guy on top, but let's not forget we all have power, and you're on *my* turf right now. You may have saddled me with the Mantle of Death, and you may have barred me from Below and Above, but don't let that go to your head. You don't own me. You never have, and let me make this abundantly clear: *you never will.*"

His eyes flicker. His hands twitch. And now we've come to the crux of the matter. Zenos' signature is wanting the things he can't have. Ever obsessed with mortal women married to other men, he never once looked my way. Not until Hadrian asked for his blessing on our union.

"How badly did it sting, Zenos? When you snuck into my bedchamber that night, and I didn't hesitate before telling

16

you to get the fuck out?"

His breathing increases. I'm pulling the tail of a dragon, but I'm beyond caring. Too long, I've endured this existence

with the knowledge it will never end. This is my fate. For denying the First of the gods in lieu of his brother, I am doomed to be ever parted from the one I love; to escort the dead to the edge of Hadrian's realm, but never to enter alongside them. I have been damned to ever remain one step away.

Because I loved another, I spurned him, and Zenos hates me for it. Out of spite and jealousy, he cursed me, and so I too, hate him. Round and round we go in an endless cycle of bitterness and rage.

It's utterly exhausting.

"Go get Mitchell Donovan. Now."

"I won't. He doesn't deserve to die. His family doesn't deserve to lose him."

"Death isn't deserved, Thana. It just is. And it's not for you to decide."

"I'm not taking him Below, Zenos. You want him that badly, go get him yourself."

"This will not end well for you, Thana, I swear it."

"Like you give a shit."

The alarm sounds, drawing both of our gazes, and breaking the standoff. Stepping around him, I draw my hood back up and grasp the scythe still balanced beside the door.

"Duty calls. You know the way out."

"Try not to let your heart get the better of you, Thana. It's gotten you into far too much trouble already."

All life drains from my gaze before I turn back to him. On a whim, I shoot an icy blast in his direction. "Fuck. You." With a twirl, I dissolve into nothing.

The days continue to pass. The dead continue to call. The sun rises and sets, and Karen and I take the few spare moments we're granted to glean any semblance of happiness we can find.

We play cards. I paint her nails. She braids my hair. In three-minute increments, we try and work our way through six seasons of *Game of Thrones*.

Life — existence — goes on.

And then the shit hits the fan.

We're at my place, for once, when the alarm goes off. I don't know why, but I'm instantly filled with an overwhelming sense of dread. Karen immediately rises and heads for my closet, but I remain glued to my seat.

"Here, I grabbed yours, too." In a moment she's back, my cloak in her hands. I don't respond; instead, I stare blankly at the wall, trying to decipher why my heart seems to have stopped.

"Thana? Thana! C'mon, we have to go."

I slowly turn to her, my dead gaze rising to meet her anxious one. "Something terrible's happened."

"Isn't it always terrible when someone dies? Let's go." She shakes my cloak in front of my face.

"No ... This is more. It's ..." I can't put words to my feeling of desolation.

"Okay, you need to snap out of it. Thana! Get up!" She clicks her fingers an inch before my eyes. When that garners no response, she slaps me. Not hard — not like Zenos — but with enough force to finally get my attention.

I stand and swing my cloak around my shoulders, moving out of habit rather than intention. Karen slides my scythe into my grip, then turns me toward the door. "Go. I'll be waiting. And whatever this feeling of yours is, I'm sure everything's fine."

"It's not fine. Someone's dead ... Someone's ..."

"Someone's always dead, Thana. Go!"

"No ... This ..."

She grabs my shoulders, then pulls me into a rough hug. "Hey. You can do this. You hear me? You have to. And I'll be here waiting, for them *and* for you. Just like always. Because we're in this together. Okay? I love you."

I know.

She disappears before I can get the words out.

I can't focus. I lose precious moments fighting my rising hysteria, trying to calm myself enough to dissipate into shadow. Finally, I fall into a state of weightlessness; moments later, I find myself standing on the edge of an operating room.

A doctor stands, bloody scalpel in hand, eyes downcast, over a garishly bright, turquoise surgical mask. Just behind lurks a monitor; a bold, red line skates across the top of the screen, accompanied by a debilitating, high-pitched screech. The lifeless frame of a stranger lies beneath a once-pristine white sheet, the fabric utterly incapable of hiding the seemingly unending pool of blood. In a far corner, another doctor cradles a motionless bundle, also sheet-covered and bloodstained.

My heart stutters.

No. Surely not this …

The leaden stillness is only an illusion; across the room, clad in blue surgical scrubs, a man flails and fights against yet another surgeon. His screams bounce off the walls and reverberate in my ears, making them ring.

"NO! No, dammit, save her! Save her, you sonofabitch! She's not dead! She's not dead! No, no, fuck, no!"

It's Mitchell Donovan.

My gaze whips back to the still form on the table, then to the tiny newborn in the doctor's arms. Realization hits hard, a ton of bricks that leaves my mind crushed and my innards shredded. Tremors seize me; I drop my scythe, and it clatters to the floor. No one looks my way. No one … except Mitch.

He doesn't see me. He can't. It's not like before …

He's not the dead one anymore.

What have I done? The thought echoes in my head, a warbling that goes on and on with no hint of ending.

No. This isn't how things are supposed to happen. They're sup-

posed to be together. They're supposed to be happy! I sent him back, I saved him! I gave him – them – a second chance. They're a family; they're supposed to get a chance to be a family! Kismet, the baby ... They're not supposed to die, dammit! This isn't fair! It's not right! No! I won't do it!

I look around for Kismet and the baby, intent on sending them back.

You can't. Look around, Thana. They've been gone for too long. The doctors have already called it.

I don't care. I sent Mitch back.

Mitch wasn't fully gone.

"I don't care!"

Again, Mitch's shouts are interrupted as he looks in my direction, searching for a sound only he can hear. When he doesn't find me, he goes back to trying to get to Kismet.

Speaking of which ... Where is she? Where is the baby? Spinning in a slow circle, I continue to search for two grey wisps, but I find nothing. *Where are they?*

"They're not here."

The scene freezes: the surgeon with the scalpel is stuck swiping a finger below his eye, the doctor carrying Mitchell's baby is mid-pivot, turning toward the door, and Mitch's mouth is stretched wide in mid-scream, his arm raised above his head and his weight thrown against the man holding him back.

I turn woodenly, my heart lodged in my throat.

Zenos.

"Where–" I cough, attempting to dislodge the dread locking my voice. "Where are they?"

"They're gone."

"Obviously. They're dead. But where are they?"

He only stares at me. I swoop down to grab my scythe and brandish it at him. "Dammit, Zenos–"

"They're with Karen. They're already on their way Below."

"How? I wasn't here, and they don't know the way. They—"

"I took them."

Stunned, I can do nothing but gape at him.

"You … You what?"

"I took them before you arrived."

"You sonofabitch. How dare you!?"

"I know you, Thana. Did you think I wouldn't know you'd try to send them back?"

"And so what if I did?"

"You can't! It's against the rules. And I don't give a fuck how much you hate me, you can't break them."

"Fuck you, Zenos. I *did* break them. I let Mitch go back, and it kills you!"

"That's not it—"

"Oh, bullshit. You're pissed that I flipped you the bird. Well, I don't give a shit. And you had no business doing my job."

"Don't bother acting all offended, Thana. You hate this job."

"Maybe so, but it's still mine!"

"You couldn't save them, Thana. You couldn't send them back."

"I could have! I sent Mitch back—"

"And look where it got him!"

Zenos' words wash over me, a lethal tsunami that burns my lungs and leaves me drowning. I look over at Mitch, still frozen in time; his face is the picture of absolute devastation, his features shattered into thousands of minute shards impossible to piece back together.

I shake my head. "No. No, this isn't my fault. It didn't have to be like this."

"You're right. It didn't."

I turn back to him, denial pouring from me. "No. I gave him a second chance. I gave them all a second chance. *This*

21

wasn't supposed to happen. I don't know how you did it, but—"

"I did nothing."

"—somehow you arranged this. To punish me. Yes, that's it. You were so furious with me. You must have wanted to teach me a lesson. That's what this is. You're teaching me a lesson, you heartless prick. You can't stand to be disobeyed, to be denied."

"Thana—"

"Is it worth it, Zenos? Is it worth destroying a family? Is it worth creating this much pain? Are you happy now? Is this enough?"

Tears are streaming down my face now; every ounce of rage and sorrow leaks from my eyes and evaporates into the air around us, charging the atmosphere and singeing us both.

"The time of their deaths is written in the stars, Thana. You know that. I don't make that call; I never have. It's never been our decision to make. But you did. *You* chose to send him back. You let your heart be swayed by love—" Sarcasm drips from his tongue. "—and you made a choice. Well, sweetheart, I'm sorry to say it, but you fucked up. If you'd taken him to Karen, let her take him Below as you were meant to, they'd all be together now."

"Except they wouldn't. I saw her future. I saw their child."

"The future isn't set in stone. You know that. Kora's an indecisive bitch; she's always pulling people's strings. You let yourself be fooled."

"Shut up."

"*You* let him go back."

"Stop it."

"*You* damned him to this existence."

"*Shut up!*"

"And now you can suffer the consequences."

He waves a hand, and Mitchell Donovan presses against the doctor holding him back. With no opposition, Mitch

22

rushes past and stumbles. Catching himself, he looks up and around, panting. His gaze falls on me.

"You!"

Fire blazes in his eyes. With an unholy yell, he races for me, his fingers curled into claws, his teeth bared in a feral growl. He launches himself, intent on tackling me, but to him I'm nothing but mist, and he flies right through me. Barreling into the wall, he collapses in a tangle of limbs.

"Zenos, stop this. He'll hurt himself!"

But Zenos is gone; he's left me alone to face the horror of what I've done.

Rising, Mitchell throws himself at me, and again hits nothing but air. His fury only grows.

I set my scythe down and raise my hands, pleading with him.

"I'm so sorry. I didn't know."

He yells as he throws a punch. The force of his swing hurls his fist through me and into the wall. He yelps in pain and cradles his hand.

"Mitchell, stop! You're going to hurt yourself."

My words do nothing but enrage him further. He goes on, trying desperately to do me physical harm; the only choice I have is to watch and wait.

Finally, he collapses into an exhausted heap on the floor. His knuckles are torn and bloody, scraps of skin hanging in ragged strips from his fingers. Beads of sweat cling to his neck and face and drip from the ends of his hair. His breath pierces his lips, sharp, jagged pants that make me wonder whether he's done some sort of internal damage to himself.

I am bleeding for him; I can't describe his pain, but I can feel every singular pinprick.

"I'm sorry, Mitch. I thought … I thought I was doing what was right."

"You told me to love my wife."

"I did."

"You told me to witness the birth of my son."

"I know."

"You didn't say their lives would be the price."

"I didn't know. Mitch, you have to believe me, I never would have—"

"You should have known! You're the Grim fucking Reaper! Isn't death supposed to be your thing? Aren't you supposed to know the rules?"

"It's not that simple. I—"

"You let them die!"

"I didn't. I swear, I didn't know. It wasn't my choice, I don't make that choice!"

"You took them from me!"

"No, I didn't. Zenos, he—"

"Get out!"

"Mitch, please! Try to understand—"

"Can you take me now?"

His words catch me off-guard. "Wh … What?"

"Can you take me with you? Can you take me to them?"

My heart shatters, because as much as I want to, I know I can't give him what he wants. Tears flow from my eyes.

"I can't."

"Why not?"

"Because … Because there are rules."

"But you broke the rules before. With me. Didn't you." It's not a question; he knows. Somehow, he knows.

"Yes. I did."

"So why can't you now?"

What am I supposed to say? There's no answer I can give him that will bring him any peace. I've destroyed him and, much as I'd like to deny it, we both know it.

"I just … can't."

He curls into himself, sobbing and shaking. I reach out to lay a hand on his shoulder, but the barrier of life separates us, and I drift through him. I can't touch him. I can't reach him.

The knowledge cuts deeply, a razor-sharp blade buried to the hilt in my gut.

"Mitchell … Please …"

"Leave me." All vestiges of anger are gone; the words are simply empty. They are all that's left of a once vibrant life razed to nothing but a dusty wasteland.

I squeeze my eyes shut and, with a slow spin, abandon him to his unjust and cruel fate.

Seconds later, I reappear on my front porch. Karen meets me at the door.

"Hey. Are you okay?"

I don't answer.

"Thana?"

I nudge past her into the living room. I barely make it to the couch before my knees give out, and I sag into the cushions.

"What happened, Thana? Zenos was here, and he—"

"I don't want to talk about it."

"But—"

"Go away, Karen."

I've never said those words to my twin. Two sides of the same coin, we've always been inseparable; she's the only source of balm to this wretched life Zenos has damned me to. But I don't want comfort now; I can't bear it.

"Thana …" She steps towards me, a hand raised.

"Go away! Get out! Just leave me alone!" I grab the nearest thing to me—a coffee cup on the end table—and hurl it at her. It passes through her and shatters against the wall.

Hurt shines from her wide eyes, but I can't find it in myself to care. I lean back against the couch, cross my arms over my chest, and stare lifelessly at the far wall.

I see nothing because there's nothing left to see.

When the alarm inevitably rings, I rise without hesitation. I don't react when the woman begs to stay. I show no sympathy when a child cries for his mother. Any effect I might once have felt is gone.

Because Death comes for us all. And though I will never die, it has finally come for me.

CAPITULATION

I stare at the array of items in front of me: my father's Glock, my prescription bottle of hydrocodone, a package of razors I bought last week, and even a dusty bit of rope I found in the neighbor's garage, though it's nowhere near long enough. It's not like I have a place to hang myself from, anyway. The scene deserves a chuckle, it's so ridiculously cliché.

But there's nothing funny about this. And it's been so long since I've smiled.

I used to. Smile, that is. Even though the depression was always a weight on my chest—some days it was damn near impossible to breathe—I still managed to grin and bear it. Maybe that's why no one ever really understood, why they still don't.

Why she doesn't.

Will she have any regrets when I'm gone? I'd like to think so, but I'm not sure I really believe it. More likely she'll be happy she has one less thing to worry about. Not as much stress on her plate.

She has no idea what stress is. None of them do.

The pain's bad—fibromyalgia's a bitch, after all—so I go ahead and pop a pill. Just one for now. It's not quite time to swallow them all. The cold water burns going down. I wince, then cough and sputter. I take another gulp, trying to calm the irritation in my throat. My eyes water, but I can breathe again. I lean back and wait for the meds to kick in.

My phone pings at me. I pick it up, swipe the screen. It's a text message from James.

"Hey. How you doing?"

I'm getting ready to off myself; that's how I'm doing. I set the phone back down, knowing I won't type those words. If I did, he'd try and stop me because unlike her, James actually cares about me. We've been friends for a couple of years now. I'm not sure how it's worked out, seeing as he's married, and I have no one in my life romantically at present. I used to, but Rick wasn't up to dealing with my issues. Not after ... But I don't want to think about that just yet. I don't blame him. Hell, it looks like even *I'm* not up to dealing with my shit anymore. But James—and his wife, for that matter—they watch out for me, and they'd be absolutely horrified if they had any inkling of what I'm about to do.

The phone goes off again.

"Hey, you okay?"

It's not like me to not answer. I know that, and so does he. He's no stranger to my depression, and if I don't respond, he'll get worried. But what can I say? I'm not okay. And if I tell him I'm not okay, he'll want to talk, and I don't want to talk anymore. I'm sick of talking. I just want to be done.

I'm feeling slightly drowsy, but the pain's still getting through, so I grab the prescription bottle and shake out another pill. It goes down easier than the first one.

After a minute, I get up and dig out a notebook and pen from my desk. I should write a note. It's customary. Expected. They'll look for a note—something that says goodbye, or at the very least provides some sort of explanation for my actions. They'll want to know.

She'll want to know.

I open the notebook, uncap the pen. A surge of fury washes over me, and I hurl the items at the wall. No. Fuck her. Fuck all of them. If they're only going to give a damn once I'm dead, maybe they should have given one sooner. Maybe she should have tried a little harder to understand, to be a little less judgmental.

Tears prick my eyes, and I sink back down on my bed. Everything's still sitting on my nightstand, all lined up in a pretty row. I reach out, grab hold of the gun. It's loaded, the rounds already racked. There's no question of whether I'll use it; it's more a matter of when and how. You'd be amazed at how many failed suicides come out of people shooting themselves. *I* certainly was when I researched it. Fifteen percent. Fifteen out of every hundred people that shoot themselves don't die.

I will not be one of them.

The fuzziness weighs a bit heavier now, and I'm a tad slower grabbing my phone when the next text message comes in.

"You're starting to scare me. Where are you?"

A few minutes later, the phone rings. Billy Boyd's voice, singing "The Last Goodbye" from *The Hobbit: Battle of the Five Armies* reaches my ears. The song is appropriate, and more than a little ironic. Needless to say, I don't answer the call. Besides, by the time James gets around to acting on his uneasiness, it'll be too late.

Setting both the gun and the phone back on the nightstand, I cross to my desk once again. Opening the browser on my computer, I pull up Netflix and turn on an episode of *Grey's Anatomy*. It's the finale of season two, where Izzy snips Denny's LVAD. I don't know why it's my favorite episode, because it's depressing as hell. I can't ever get through it without crying, even after ten years and God knows how many viewings.

But watching anything that *isn't* depressing seems wrong; there's something off about killing yourself while watching something that at one point would have made you laugh. As the show goes on, I down a couple more pills.

Suddenly, I want a beer. Which is weird; because I don't drink beer. But I feel like I ought to have one—a celebratory toast to my life, as it were, in spite of how fucked up it is. I stand and head for the door. I'm pretty sure there's a few in the fridge. I have no idea how old they are; Rick brought them with one of the last times he stayed over, and that was months ago. Whatever. They'll work.

I stumble into the kitchen. The meds have kicked in. I'm a

touch unsteady on my feet. Doesn't matter. Once I get back to my room I have a feeling I won't be getting back up again. I open the fridge, peer inside. I shove the milk carton and some yogurt to the side.

There! Three bottles of Shiner Bock, with their mustard yellow labels bearing a ram's head. I pull one out, let the fridge door swing closed. I need a bottle opener. I spin in a slow circle, my mind hazy. Opening drawers at random, I finally find one with the rest of my utensils. I put it to the cap, wrench up. The opener slips.

"Shit!"

I've sliced my finger open. It's bleeding, but I don't really feel it. I should probably rinse it off and slap a bandage on it, but what's the point, really? Setting the beer on the counter I try again. This time the cap pops off, and I take a swig.

The hoppy bitterness swims over my tongue and burns my throat going down. My stomach roils, and I struggle not to sputter or gag. How did Rick ever drink this shit? In spite of the nausea, I bring the bottle back to my lips. After another sip or two, I sway back to my room, letting my hand trail against the wall. An illusion of stability. I snort. My life's anything but stable; it seems fitting as I stumble along that precariousness should play witness to its end.

Passing the bathroom, I pause. I think I'll pee now. Maybe then I won't wet myself so badly when I die. That happens, you know. When you die your bowels go lax and anything that's in there comes out. They never seem to mention that on the television shows. Dead bodies on screen, though grotesque, tend to be unusually clean. God forbid the public be forced to face reality.

I slide my pants off and collapse onto the toilet.

Reality's ugly. That's why they never depict it on-screen. Because no one wants to watch something that hits too close to home.

I listen to the steady stream of urine, then fumble with the roll of toilet paper. It takes three or four tries before I manage to get a decent handful. I wipe, rise, flush. I don't bother putting my pants back on. Too much effort. Besides, I won't be needing them where I'm going—wherever that is.

I make it back to my bedroom. My vision's fuzzy. I know I shouldn't put my head down, but I'm so tired. I'll only rest for a minute or two. Then I'll get back to business.

My head hits the pillow. Shapes swirl in front of my eyes. The sound of Meredith and Christina's voices morph and shift. The walls melt away …

" — your fault! You weren't watching him enough! If you'd paid better attention, this wouldn't have happened!"

"That's not fair, Mom! I did —"

"You didn't! I asked so little of you. All I needed you to do was keep an eye on him, make sure he took his meds, make sure he ate."

"I did all that —"

"It really wasn't that much to ask. You dropped out of school. Then you lost your job. It was the least you could do in return for my putting you up."

"Putting me up? This is my home, too, Mom, it's —"

"You should have been out of here forever ago! You're twenty-two years old, dammit! I should have put my foot down and made you find your own place. I should have known you weren't responsible enough to handle your father. I should have just hired a nurse and been done with it."

"Mom, please! You didn't need a nurse, and I did watch him. Dad was sick! He was sick, and this was always going to happen. You know that. The doctor said —"

"It didn't have to happen now. He could have had another ten years. Maybe more. But because of you, he's dead. You killed him. You killed your father!"

"No! God, please Mom, don't say that! I didn't. I never wanted this to happen. I loved him, Mom, just like you!"

"Get out!"

The scene shifts, and he's there, feet up in his recliner. I

31

stand beside him, a glass full of water in one hand and a collection of pills in the other.

"Hey, Daddy, how you doing?"

"Okay."

"Yeah? You feeling alright?"

"Yeah. I'm feeling pretty good, actually."

"That's good. I'm glad. Here. It's time for your meds."

"Yep. Seems to be about that time, doesn't it?"

He tosses the pills in, takes a drink, swallows, and then wipes his hand across his mouth.

"I need to go to the store later. That okay?"

"Sure, Dad. Just let me know when, and I'll drive you."

"Thanks, honey."

"Sure thing. And you've got a doctor's appointment tomorrow, right?"

"Yeah, I think so. At ten, I think."

"Okay. I'll make sure I'm ready to go."

"Sounds good. You got any plans for tonight? You going out with Rick or anything like that?"

"Rick and I broke up, Dad. Remember?"

"You did? Oh, yeah, that's right. I remember now. I'm sorry, sweetie."

"No problem."

"Well, he's an asshole. And so is any guy who thinks my baby's not good enough for him."

"I love you, Daddy."

"I love you, too, sweetheart."

His recliner twists and contorts, flattening into a rectangular box lined in a light navy satin. He's lying inside. His eyes are closed, and his face is covered in a thin sheet of make-up. His hands are crossed above his navel, stiff and cold.

"What are you doing here? I told you not to come."

"He's my father."

"Yes. He is. And it's your fault he's dead."

"Mom, please, don't make a scene here. Dad wouldn't want it."

"Don't lecture me about what your father would have wanted. Your father would have wanted to live. He would have wanted to stay here, with me."

"We all want to stay here, Mom. For as long as we can. But we don't always get to make that choice."

"No, we don't. And in this case, you made it for him."

"Stop this."

"You weren't watching him."

"Mom – "

"You left him alone."

"It was an accident – "

"You killed him!"

The slap catches me off-guard, the sharp crack echoing in the quiet room. The murmured chatter dies. Pairs of shocked eyes all shoot in our direction. I lift my hand to my burning cheek, unshed tears stinging my eyes. I look for her, but she's not in front of me anymore. Now she's sitting next to me, her hand gripping mine. Her eyes brim with tears of her own.

"You're sure, doctor?"

"Yes. I'm very sorry."

"But, Alzheimer's ... He won't be able to work. He won't be able to ... How will he ...? Oh God, what are we supposed to do?

"Right now his condition isn't terribly advanced, but it will worsen over time, and unfortunately, there's no way to stop the deterioration of his mind. We just haven't progressed that far. For now, he'll probably be lucid more often than not, but as time goes on, he will have longer and more frequent periods of dementia. The pattern of those periods may also fluctuate; at times he may remember who you are, but not where he is. At other times he may think you're someone else, or not know you at all. Most likely he will experience episodes where he has lost track of time and is reliving something that has happened in his past. The most important thing for you both to remember is to try and keep him as calm as possible. If he sees you getting frustrated or upset, or if you get overly flustered trying to convince him of something, it will only make his situation

33

worse. His sense of reality is going to shift exceptionally, possibly from day to day."

"So we won't know when we wake up each morning how he might be."

"That's correct. His daily reality will continually shift as the disease accelerates. Eventually, however, it is my belief that he will reach a state where he will no longer remember anything of his current life. His moments of lucidity will be extremely rare, if they happen at all."

"Oh, God!"

"I'm sorry. The nature of Alzheimer's is cruel. It is not an easy disease to handle. I don't like having to suggest it, but you might want to consider putting him in a home where he can receive professional care."

"No, I don't want to do that."

"Mrs. Fowler, I understand you want to do what's best for him, but —"

"I'm not going to put him in a home! He'd feel so betrayed by that, so hurt! I can't do that to him, I can't!"

"Mrs. Fowler —"

"NO!"

For the first time since the doctor uttered the word "Alzheimer's," I speak up.

"I'll watch him."

They both look at me.

"What?"

"I'll look after him, Mom. I'll be Dad's caretaker."

"But...what about school?"

"I can finish school anytime. This is more important. Besides, it'll be good practice."

"And your job?"

"I'll manage. And if it gets to be too much, I'll ask for a leave of absence. Or I'll quit. Whatever it takes. I know putting Dad in a home would kill you, and you've got enough to worry about. So don't. I'll stay with him. I'll take care of him, for as long as I can."

"*You'll stay with him?*"

"*Yes.*"

"*You'll keep him safe?*"

"*I promise, Mom.*"

She looks at the doctor, an eyebrow raised in question. He shrugs, then leans forward and rests his folded hands on his desk.

"*I see no issue with it for now. But please understand that a time may come where it will be best for him to have professional care.*"

"*I understand, Doctor. You'll excuse me, though, for praying that day never comes.*"

We leave the room hand-in-hand and head for the hospital stairs. Reaching the top, I'm suddenly alone, and when I look down, my father is crumpled in a heap at the bottom.

"*Dad? Daddy!*"

I race down the stairs, falling to my knees at his side.

"*God, no! Dad!*"

I feel for a pulse. There isn't one.

"*No, no, no! Daddy, please!*"

Shaking, I yank my phone from my pocket. It clatters to the floor. I pick it up, manage to punch in three digits. I don't remember speaking. But within minutes, I hear sirens. I watch, frozen, as paramedics rush past me. Muttered phrases slip through my ears, but don't truly register. *Broken neck. Dead on arrival. Nothing can be done.*

"*Ma'am? Ma'am. Do you know what happened? Ma'am!*"

"*He must have fallen. I don't know. He's not supposed to be upstairs. What was he doing upstairs?*"

My mother's voice blends with my own.

"*What was he doing upstairs? What were you doing upstairs?*"

"*I don't know, Mom. He must have tried to follow me, but I don't know why. I was only up there for a second, I – *"

"*Why were you up there at all?*"

"*He wanted you guys' wedding afghan. He kept asking for it, saying he needed it. He was getting agitated, and I couldn't get him*" redirected. He kept trying to get up, telling me he was going to go find it. I told him I would go get it for him if he would just stay put. I knew where it was; it would only take me a second to run upstairs and get it from the hope chest. I made him promise he would stay where he was, and he did. He promised."

"You know you can't trust him. The doctor told us that!"

"I know, Mom! But I was only gone a minute. I don't even know how he got up the stairs that fast. I was just closing the hope chest and getting ready to come back down when I heard the crash. It was only a minute, I swear."

"You shouldn't have gone. You shouldn't have left him alone!"

"It was the only thing I could think to do. I didn't think it would hurt anything."

"Well, you thought wrong, didn't you!? You killed him!"

"I killed him."

My words are slurred. My face and the pillow beneath are soaked with tears. My phone rings again, then pings. And pings again. And once more. The phone slips from my fingers and clatters to the floor. *Where …?* My arm dangles off the bed, my hand sweeping along the rough carpet. The tips of my fingers tingle. Finally, I grab it and somehow manage to open my inbox.

The words swim in front of my eyes; letters line up in no apparent order, with pieces of punctuation spattered in. My head pounds as I squint and struggle to make sense of whatever rant James is on.

"Where the hell are you?"

"Answer me, dammit!"

"If I don't hear from you in the next five minutes, I'm coming over."

I let the phone fall beside me, then rub my eyes, trying to banish the fog hanging so heavily over my head. So that's it. I'm out of time. James lives about fifteen minutes away, which gives me about a twenty minute window. Not a lot of time, but enough.

It takes three attempts, but I eventually manage to sit up. I reach for the pill bottle. I struggle with the cap, fighting to add enough pressure to get it to twist. Finally it comes off and lands on the carpet with a soft thud. I raise my shaking arm, bring the bottle to my mouth, and pour the rest of the pills in. I look around for the beer. It's gone, and I wonder if I left it in the bathroom. I must have. So I grab the water, now tepid, and gulp it down. As I swallow, the glass slips from my fingers and falls to the floor. The remaining water splashes and seeps into the carpet.

Next, I rip the package of razors open. It's difficult—the hydrocodone is quickly taking hold. Honestly, the meds are probably enough. But if James finds me passed out on painkillers, there's a chance they'll pump my stomach and revive me. I can't allow that to happen.

I drop the first razor, and I'm too lightheaded to try and pick it up, so I yank the next one from the package. Slipping the guard off, I lay the blade along the skin of my wrist and jerk, making a swift, jagged, horizontal cut. Something whispers to me that I should have cut vertically. *The artery lies vertically beneath the skin.* I know that. My textbooks told me so. Then again, I don't want to bleed out so fast I can't finish what I've started. I switch the razor to my other hand and make another clumsy slice.

Blood flows down my hands, oozing over my fingers, and pooling on my bed. Nothing hurts anymore, and for the first time in what feels like forever, I smile.

I should be scared. I'm dying, after all. But all I feel is a sense of relief. The pain is gone; I don't have to live with it anymore. I can finally be at peace.

My vision is growing black, and I know I'm on the edge of losing consciousness. Reaching out, I clasp the Glock and hug it close to my chest.

"I'm coming, Dad."

All of a sudden, I'm five years old, and he's there. I'm

standing on his feet, raised up on my toes, and we're dancing. With a laugh, he swings me up into his arms and spins. Then he plants a wet, slobbery kiss on my cheek, and I giggle.

Raising his gun, I put it to my temple. Covered in blood, it's slippery in my grasp, so I tighten my hold. My breath is shallow; focusing one last time, I suck in a deep breath.

Below me, I hear a frantic pounding on the front door, along with muffled shouts. Floating above the noise, a quiet whisper tickles my ear.

"I'm waiting for you, sweetheart."

I grin and pull the trigger.

PREY

There was no easing back into reality. No drifting through the fog of the in-between. It was abrupt. Jarring. A sharp jerk into what should have been light.

Her eyes shot open. Her heart hammered, slamming the sharp nails of her breath into her ribs. Her muscles cramped, nerves barraging her skin like a firing squad, her fight-or-flight response jammed into fifth gear. Except there was no one to strike. Nowhere to run.

Darkness enveloped her.

Not the dark of the streets, where headlights and lamps provided pools of illumination every few feet, keeping the demons — God-willing — at bay. Not the dark of her bedroom, where the slats of her blinds created moonlit shadows, barely guiding her to the adjoining bathroom door. Not even the dark of the thickest portions of Forest Park, where the moon's beams still managed to filter through the heavy foliage.

This was darkness to the tenth degree. Black. Pitch. Impossible to see her hand an inch in front of her face.

Where am I?

She whipped her head from side to side, tried to roll. Her pulse pelted her carotid, bruising her neck. She screamed, but whatever held her captive swallowed the sound. She tried again. And again. Finally, when her lungs wheezed and her throat burned, she stopped.

No one was coming. No one could hear.

Closing her eyes, she let her other senses go to work. Her ears told her nothing. The silence was as heavy as the darkness, weighing her down. Crushing her. In opposition to the pressure, she pulled air into her lungs, dragged it, forced it to expand. *Mildew.* Accompanied by stale mustiness. The smell was nursing home, laced with hospital, with a touch of dusty attic. *A basement?*

She focused in on her body. Her hands brushed against something soft, but rough. Ratty. *A Berber carpet?* No. Not quite. Her fingers curled, digging in. *What is this?* Raising her hand up, she ran into another surface, only inches above her head. She couldn't sink and curl her fingers into this; instead, it gave way when she pressed it, then bounced back. Plush.

Letting her hands travel as far as possible in one direction, then the other, she came across a fissure almost directly above her head. Whatever she was in, it had indeed been cut; she could feel the crude stitches where someone had sewn it shut. She tore at them until the searing pain of a ripped fingernail had her cursing. She brought her middle finger to her mouth, sucked, tasted the metallic sting of blood.

What is going on? Where am I? And why? The questions circled relentlessly in her mind. Panic rose, threatened to overtake her again. She shook her head, trying to fight it back. She couldn't win. With desperate cries, she clawed furiously at the stitches. More nails snagged and split, the remains jagged and bleeding. Lost in a whirl of terror, she hardly noticed.

Time had no meaning as she struggled. Eventually, exhaustion won out, dragging her into oblivion.

Something's different. Her eyes fluttered open, adjusting to the light.

Light!

She glanced around, searching for its source, and made out the blurred lines of whatever held her captive. And when she lifted her hand, there were her five fingers, the tattered nails more than evident.

She looked up, beyond her hand. She could see them. Barely. The line of sutures that locked her in. She reached for them, then froze as a door slammed. Footsteps. Heavy ones.

And … *Creaking? Stairs?* Should she call out? Yell for help? Instinct warned her help wasn't coming, not from whoever was clomping nearer. There was no hesitation in those steps, no consideration. Only determination.

She laid her hands back down. Closed her eyes. Waited. She felt a tug above her, and heard the click of something metallic. The light against her eyelids grew. She cracked them open, peeked through the slit. *Someone is cutting the stitches!* She slammed her lids shut again, held her breath. *No. That's a giveaway! Breathe normally, dammit! In, out. In, out. Otherwise, they'll realize I know they're here.*

The fissure grew. The scissors ceased. She could hear whoever it was now. Breathing. Panting.

"I know you're awake."

The voice was deep, steady, slightly amused. She didn't open her eyes.

"Suit yourself."

Rough hands slid under her shoulders and knees. Her captor grunted, then lifted. She forced herself to remain limp. Moments later, lanky arms laid her out. She sank into what she assumed could only be a bed. Goosebumps popped against her skin. *No. This can't be happening.*

"Open your eyes." Now the voice grew soft, gentle. "Please."

A request. Not a command.

She denied him.

"I said, open your eyes!" Now the command came, angry and shrill, accompanied by a slap that left her eardrums ringing.

The strike launched her into action. Her eyelids flew open, her gaze finding her assailant, registering only that he was tall and lean. She threw herself at him, fingers curled, torn nails exposed. She raked her fingernails down his face, drawing blood.

"Bitch!"

The furious expletive reverberated in her ears. She winced, hesitated. Big mistake. He was on her, and he was stronger than he looked. She fought, struggling, crying out, doing anything she could to get away. Unexpectedly, he let her go. She didn't know why, she didn't care, she just ran. Tears streaming down her face, she tripped up the steps — *It is a basement* — finally, finally reached the door. She tugged, but it was locked.

No! Dammit, no! Stupid, fucking door!

"Let me out! Oh, God, please, somebody open the door!"

A burning sensation pierced her arm. She looked down. A syringe stood erect, the needle buried deep in her skin. *Wha ...?* She went limp, falling into waiting arms. Back down the stairs. Back on the bed. She tried to move, but couldn't. Her mind, however, was alert as ever.

Ketamine. He drugged me with ketamine.

"Why did you do that?" He stood in front of her, hands on his hips, head dipped. "Why did you make me hurt you? I don't want to hurt you."

He looked up, looked directly at her. Her mind recoiled at the combination of regret and adoration in his eyes, the sincerity in his voice. He'd kidnapped her, held her captive, drugged her! And now he looked at her like ... like this?

"I love you, Kelly. Please don't make me hurt you again."

He knows my name. Oh God, he knows my name! Nausea rose up, choking her.

"Wh ... who ... are you?" She could barely croak the words out.

"Don't tease me, Kelly. You know who I am."

"N ... no ... I ... don ..."

"Kelly." His tone was tinged with anguish. He raced over to the side of the bed, fell to his knees beside her. "Don't be mean. You're always being mean. Always playing hard to get. But I know. I know you love me, too. I've seen the coy looks you send me when you think I'm not looking. I've heard the hints in your voice. You don't have to hide the way you feel anymore. You're here now. You're with me. Now we can be together."

She wanted to shake her head; instead, it just lolled to the side. Her gut clenched as she watched his hands go to his belt. *No. God, please, no. Not this.*

His pants slid to the floor.

This can't be happening.

His hands were at her hips.

"Plea … pl …"

"Shh. It'll be okay, Kelly. I won't hurt you. I love you. So much."

Unable to do anything else, she clamped her eyes shut, and endured.

When it was over, he climbed off of her, careful not to put any weight on her limp body. He crossed the room, disappeared through a door, then returned with a wet cloth. Gently, he swiped it over her body, rinsing away the remnants of what he'd done to her.

"Are you okay, Kelly? It was good, wasn't it?"

She didn't answer.

"Please say something. Tell me it was good. Tell me you're okay. I need to know you're okay."

Are you kidding? Okay? She'd never be okay again.

"Dammit, Kelly! Why do you do this to me? Ignore me, when I know you have feelings for me! I see the way you watch me. You want to be here. You want this, you want me! I know you do!"

Still, she remained silent.

"Damn you! You stupid bitch!"

And then he was hitting her, backhanding her again and again. It should have hurt. It must have hurt. But the ketamine was still in full effect, keeping her anesthetized. Her lack of response seemed to enrage him. Swiping his belt from the floor, he wrapped it around his fist, and let loose. The leather lashed at her skin, against her thighs, her abdomen, her exposed breasts.

She'd read about dissociative experiences in class, heard her professors describe them. Now, she experienced one. Drifting, she floated along the ceiling, staring down at herself. At him. Detached, she studied herself. Her lip was split. Her right eye had swollen shut. Welts popped up in a chaotic pattern of red stripes against her skin. When the drug wore off, she was going to be a ball of agony. For now, though? She felt nothing.

What if he overdosed me? Could I get that lucky? Perhaps consciousness would abandon her. Maybe she'd fall asleep and never wake up from this horror. Something told her that hope was futile.

Finally, after what seemed like a lifetime, he stopped. Dropping the belt, he sobbed.

"I'm sorry. I'm so sorry, Kelly, I didn't mean it, I swear. Oh God, I didn't mean it!"

He collapsed beside her on the bed, gathered her close in his arms, his streaming tears mingling with her own.

"Forgive me. Please, forgive me. I won't do it again, I swear. Please don't hate me."

Too late.

When she showed signs of having the feeling return to her limbs, he lifted her, carried her back across the room, and laid her in what had held her captive: a mattress. Next to it, a thick comforter and pillows lay haphazardly.

"No. Don ... don't put me back ..." The drugs were wearing off, but it was still difficult to speak.

"Don't worry, Kelly. It won't always be like this. But I have to keep you safe." And he slid her down, into the mattress' innards.

"No."

She tried to sit up, but pain blossomed throughout her torso. She moaned, fell back. Then the split top of the mattress closed over her, and a hefty needle, threaded with thick twine, pierced the material, back and forth, until a long line of stitches sealed the gap.

"I'll be back later, Kelly. I love you."

His footsteps receded, stomping up the stairs. A door clicked distantly. Without warning, darkness — blindness — descended.

She woke in her own room. Sunlight filtered through the blinds, the leaves on the oak outside her window shining bright and green. She looked around, confused. *What ...? This isn't right, is it?* Her nursing textbooks lay haphazardly on her desk. Family pictures covered the walls. Dirty clothes over-flowed from her laundry hamper. Relaxing, she heaved a sigh of relief. The sheets rustled next to her, the waterbed mattress swaying and pitching, and the sense of calm vanished. Her heart plummeted into her gut. *Shit, he's here! He's in my room!*

"Morning, lover."

Except it was John. Her boyfriend of two years. He turned towards her, his red hair ruffled and standing out in tufts. He gave her a sleepy grin, yawned, stretched his arms over his head.

She could only stare at him. *What is he doing here? What am I doing here?* She could have sworn she'd been in a basement, trapped in a mattress, at the mercy of a stranger. For days. She was missing. Her mother would be worried. John would be worried. Yet here he was, lying in her bed, looking at her as if nothing was amiss.

He propped himself up on an elbow, gave her a quizzical look. "Hey, you okay?"

"Yeah ..." She glanced around, gave herself a mental shake. *Snap out of it, Kelly.* It had all been a bad dream, appar-ently. She should be grateful, not trying to reason it all out. "What day is it?"

"You must have been out hard, huh?" He laughed at her,

reached out to run a finger down her cheek. "It's Tuesday."

Tuesday. She had Anatomy IV and Pathology II on Tuesdays. She swung her legs over the side of the bed, prepared to rise.

"Hey, where you going?" John reached out, pulled her back into bed. Waves rolled beneath them, adding a natural undulation to their linked bodies.

She gave a slight tug of half-hearted resistance. "I've got to get ready for class. Besides, my mom's probably cooking

breakfast downstairs, and she'll wonder if I don't come down."

"Kelly, your mom's known about you and me for months. I even talked to her about it."

"You did? When?"

"A few months ago. I told her I was sleeping with her daughter, but that I wasn't just looking for a piece of ass. I told her I loved you very much, that I would never hurt you, and I asked if it would be a problem if I stayed over every now and again, because, if so, I didn't want to disrespect her by sleeping with you under her roof. Though it wasn't going to stop me from doing so under mine, as long as you were amenable."

"You so did not say that!"

"Wanna bet?

"You said 'amenable'?"

"Sure did. She told me she was very impressed by my vocabulary. She also gave me her blessing."

She punched his shoulder. "Why didn't you tell me?"

"Because it's fun to sneak around. And you're so cute when you're trying to be quiet."

She wanted to be offended. She even tried to act like she was. John wasn't fooled. He rolled her under him, leaned down to kiss her.

"John, seriously, I have to get to class."

"I'll be quick. Promise."

Slipping a hand between their bodies, he found her clit, began to rub. She was wet in moments. He positioned himself, thrust into her. Her eyes fell shut. She moaned, lifted her hips to meet his. In moments, he was panting.

Something's not right. John didn't pant. He moaned.

"I love you, Kelly. So much. Tell me you love me, too. Oh, Kelly, I love you. I love you. I love you."

No. This is wrong. John told her he loved her, but not like this. Not now. It was always after making love, never during. And his voice … His voice was wrong. No longer John's sweet tenor, the tragically familiar voice deepened.

Horrified, she looked up. John was gone. Now, it was *him*, pumping into her, sweat from his forehead dripping onto her bare breasts. Her gaze shot around. Natural light no longer streamed through her window; now it glowed harshly from the light fixture above their heads. Her room was gone. She was back in the basement, back with him.

It had all been an illusion, a cruel trick of her broken mind, daring to hope when there was nothing left to hope for.

She came awake suddenly, her breath sawing in her chest. There was nothing there, no one to see. She was alone, sewn into her mattress, destined to wait for her rapist's return. Despair washed over her, and she embraced it. Sinking down, she thought of her mother, of John, of her life that had been irrevocably altered. When the tears came, she didn't deny them. She conceded to wretchedness, and wept.

Days passed. She didn't know how many. Incessant darkness paired with intermittent hallucinations made it impossible to keep track. The only regularity was his visits, and even those had lost their sense of reality. She could never be completely sure if he was really there, or if her nightmares had conjured him. Still, she assumed it had been nearly a month.

He would bring her meals. Escort her to the adjoining

47

bathroom so she could relieve herself. Sometimes, he'd leave her long enough she couldn't hold it. When that happened, he'd give her just enough ketamine to keep her docile. Then he'd fill the tub with warm water, set her in, and gently scrub her clean, apologizing all the while for being kept away so long. There was nothing he could do about the mattress, however, and she was sure the last thing she'd ever smell was the scent of her own stale urine. He'd long since given up on keeping her dressed; the only things covering her now were the ever-changing, colored bruises from his fists and the red welts from his belt.

Every day, he raped her. If she struggled, he drugged her. If she insulted him, he slapped her. If she said nothing at all, he beat the shit out of her.

More than anything, he told her he loved her. It made her sick.

It was also her only advantage.

"Good morning, Kelly."

"Hey, baby."

She stared at him through the torn sutures as he lifted her from the mattress and set her on her feet. He always returned her there; as much freedom as she'd managed to gain, she still hadn't convinced him to leave her free and unattended.

Smart boy.

Out of habit, she perused her surroundings as she walked to the bathroom. Nothing had changed; nothing ever did. Except … *Wait a minute!* Her gaze caught on what appeared to be a small safe. The door was open, and inside … *Are those syringes?* She faltered.

"What's wrong, Kelly?"

"Nothing. Sorry, I just tripped over my own two feet. I'm a little stiff."

"Are you alright?"

"Yeah, baby, I'm fine."

She slipped into the bathroom, shutting the door behind her. Her mind whirled. *Syringes! The ketamine! This could be my chance!* Even if they were empty, she could still use one as weapon. It would give her a few seconds, surely. *Wait. What about the door? Does he keep it locked?* Did he have keys for it? Were they on him? And if they were, did she have any way to get them from him? No. Not if he wasn't drugged. Besides, the syringes were most likely empty. *Except, he always drugs me so quickly. He never has time to actually draw the drug from a vial. Does he?* Whatever. She'd worry about the door when she got to it.

And if I don't get away? She'd lose what little trust she'd garnered from him. And the beating … The beating she'd get would be brutal. But what choice did she have? To stay here forever, pretending to love her rapist? Calling him baby? Hoping against hope someday he'd let her out of this godforsaken basement and out into the world? *Fuck that.* She'd take the beating.

She gazed at her reflection for a long moment. She didn't recognize the stranger looking back at her. Chestnut hair hung in limp tangles around a gaunt, drawn face. Barely a spark of life glinted from the dull stare. Circles of exhaustion gave the illusion of permanent black eyes, and a perpetually swollen bottom lip hinted at some sort of crude and unintentional sensuality.

Is this who I am now? Who I'm content to be? Some gangly stray he kicks around or strokes depending on his mood? Dear God, what has he done to me?

Lifting her hands up, she pushed her hair back from her face. Scrubbed her eyes. Took a deep breath. She could do this. She *had* to do this. Hurriedly, she took care of her business, then, with a mental shake, opened the door.

"I missed you." She slid into his arms, letting her body melt against his, raising her lips to press against his mouth.

His surprise was there in the slight hesitation before returning her embrace; she never initiated contact. The evidence of his approval jutted against her belly. His arms tightened around her. His tongue thrust into her mouth.

She fought the urge to resist. Forced herself to remain lax and willing in his hold. *Chill out, Kelly. Just relax. You can do this.* She kissed him back, sucking on his tongue, letting her own tangle with his. He moaned, then lifted her off her feet and headed for the bed. She ran her tongue along the length of his neck, stopping to suck the spot where his pulse pounded. He dropped her onto the bed, then fell atop her, pressing her into the softness.

"No, baby. Wait." She laid her hands on his shoulders, pushed. He looked at her, anger flashing briefly in his eyes. She leaned up, kissed him in reassurance. "I want to do something different this time."

He shook his head and tried to kiss her again. She turned away, pushed again. "Please, baby. Trust me." When he looked at her again, she plunged. "I love you. Let me show you. Let me show you how much I love you."

The words worked. He relaxed, letting her roll him to his back. Forcing the ball of nausea in her stomach away, she straddled him, slipped her hands under his shirt, let her hands roam over his bare chest. He reached for her, but she evaded him.

"Shh. Relax. You know I love you, baby. Just let me love you."

He lay back, his eyes slamming shut, his hands falling away. This was going to work. *If I can go through with it.* She had to go through with it.

Her fingers found the fly of his pants. Working the button first, then the zipper, she slid her hand inside and freed his erection. The sight of it sickened her. *How am I going to do this? I can't do this!*

Panic threatened; she pushed it away. *Think about John.*

Just imagine it's John. She didn't want to. It wasn't fair, wasn't right to bring something so good, so bright, into a place this dark. John didn't belong here.

Neither do I.

He would forgive her. If he knew what she was about to do, John would forgive her. He wouldn't hate her for using him to get through it. She had to believe that.

Closing her eyes, she let everything fall away. The putrid walls bled into the sky blue of her bedroom. Windows appeared, letting light filter in. The mattress beneath her began to sway and pitch, morphing into the waves of her waterbed. And the facade of a lover beneath her became the love of her life.

Sliding down the length of his legs, she found him with her mouth. She licked the tip of his penis, circled it with her tongue, teasing it. Then she ran her tongue along his length, back and forth. Slowly. Ever so slowly. He groaned. Bucked. She let her mouth hover just above him, building his anticipa tion. Finally, she took him into her mouth, and sucked. Up and down, back and forth, she found a rhythm he seemed to like.

"Kelly. Oh God, Kelly!" His hands fisted in her hair, holding her still, and his hips took over. He pumped into her mouth, thrusting again and again, his breath coming in harsh pants.

Stay calm. Keep your jaw relaxed. It's almost over.

Harder thrusts. Faster pants.

C'mon. Just come. Come, damn you!

He came. Semen spurted down her throat. She swallowed, forcing herself to get him through the entire orgasm. *Enjoy it while you can, asshole.* When he finally fell limp, she sprang.

Leaping off the bed, she dashed for the safe.

"Wha … Kelly?"

She dropped to her knees, hands fumbling in the safe. *Hurry. Hurry!*

51

"Kelly? Where'd you go?"

Her fingers closed around a syringe. It was drawn up.

"Kelly! What are you doing?"

She turned. He was sitting up, legs hanging over the side of the bed, pants still undone. She paused, fascinated by the change of expression morphing his features: sexual satisfaction, confusion, realization, rage.

His anger triggered her own. Uncapping the syringe, she charged him, screaming.

"You son of a bitch!" He tried to ward her off, but she'd caught him off-guard. She swung out with the syringe, burying the needle deep in his neck. She depressed the plunger, shooting the drug home. The effect was immediate. His eyes glazed over. His limbs went limp. He slid off the bed into a heap on the floor.

She stood above him, syringe still in hand, gasping. *I did it.*

Relief washed over her, and along with it all the terror, fury, hatred, and hurt she'd endured for so many days.

She kicked him as hard as she could. In the belly. In the head. In the groin. Over and over, she kicked and kicked and kicked, railing at him the whole time.

"You fucking son of a bitch, I hate you. I hate you. I hate you! I hope you burn in hell, you lousy, stupid, fucking son of a bitch! I hate you!"

Tears streamed down her face. Her lungs burned. Reason returned.

She had to go. *Now.*

She glanced around frantically. *Her clothes.* What had he done with her clothes? She burst into the bathroom, opened the cabinet beneath the sink. Nothing. She ran back into the outer room. She looked beneath both beds, searched the safe, peered under the stairs. She couldn't find them anywhere.

Looking back at him, she hesitated. The last thing she wanted to do was touch him. But she couldn't run down the streets naked. *Buck up, Kelly. You've come this far. Finish it, before the ketamine wears off.* She hurried over to him, unbuttoned his shirt, somehow managed to shift his dead weight around so the sleeves slipped free. Throwing it on, she buttoned it back up with shaky fingers. For the first time, she was thankful he was so tall; the shirt tails hung nearly to her knees. Then, she muscled his belt free from his pants, looped it around her waist, tightened it.

It was crude, on the verge of lewd, but it was better than nothing.

Turning away, she raced for the stairs. Stumbling up them, she reached the door and twisted the knob. The door didn't budge. *What the hell?* She twisted again, harder, and threw her body against the door. Still, she remained trapped. *Oh no. God, please no!* She couldn't get this far and not make it. It wasn't fair! She beat her fists against the wood, sobbing, begging anyone who might listen to let her go. Reaching down, she gripped the knob, working it back and forth, hoping against hope it might work its way free.

I'm going to die here. The ketamine's going to wear off, and he's going to come up here and get me, and then he'll kill me. Or he'll put me back in that mattress. I don't want to go back into that mattress!

Filled with frustration and despair, she screamed. The shrill shriek burned her throat and set her ears ringing. She heard him groan and try to murmur her name.

No. No, dammit! I am not dying here!

She took a deep breath, forcing her lungs to expand, and beat the panic back. Turning back to the door, she studied it for a moment; realization was a facepalm to the forehead.

It's locked.

Fumbling with the latch, she flipped it, then turned the knob. The door sprang free, and she stumbled out into a hallway. She looked right, then left. The front door beckoned.

Without another thought, she ran.

"I need to call the police."

The woman behind the counter — her name tag said Victoria—didn't even bother to look up. "I'm sorry. We're not allowed to let customers use the phone."

Is she kidding? "Did you not hear me? I don't want to make a fucking social call, lady."

Her use of profanity must have been enough to drag Victoria's eyes from the page of Vogue, or whatever magazine she was engrossed in. Her eyes widened, and she quickly gave Kelly a once-over, then glanced around; every customer's eyes were glued to the pair of them. Victoria fidgeted uncomfortably. "Ma'am, if you could please keep your voice down ..."

"Call the fucking police!" Kelly knew she was creating a scene, but didn't care. *Let them all gawk and stare. Let them think I'm crazy. I just want this to be over.*

"Okay, alright, please, just keep your voice down."

She reached for the phone, then lifted the receiver to her ear. Kelly lunged across the counter and tore it from her hand. Victoria started to protest. Kelly shot her a murderous glare.

"Dial. Nine one one. Now."

Kelly heard three beeps as Victoria dialed, followed by a professional male voice.

"Nine one one, what's your emergency?"

"I need the police. I've been raped."

Three months. She'd been missing for three months. Her mother, Donna, reported her missing when she didn't come home after a late shift at work. The cops did what they could; they questioned her friends and family members, checked the video footage from the restaurant where she was working immediately before her disappearance, posted flyers, alerted the neighboring jurisdictions. Nothing had broken.

Obviously.

Sitting beneath fluorescent lights in a white paper gown, she tried desperately to ignore the nurse, Nancy, swabbing her vagina. The swoosh of the curtain being pulled back drew her attention.

"Kelly Johnson?"

"Yes."

"Oh, I'm sorry. I didn't realize ..." The stranger in uniform gestured toward the nurse, then stepped back and pulled the curtain closed again. After a moment, Nancy finished. She lowered Kelly's gown, lifted the bedsheet over Kelly's legs, then poked her head around the curtain and invited the officer back in.

"Hi, Kelly, I'm Officer Franko, from the St. Louis Police Department. Can I talk to you about what happened?"

About what happened. It sounded so generic. So unremarkable. Like the last three months of her life hadn't been ripped from her, leaving her utterly wasted and irrevocably changed.

"Kelly?"

She stared at him. He was completely unlike the man who'd held her hostage. Dark where he'd been light. Brawny where he'd been lithe. Good where he'd been bad ... hopefully.

"If you'd be more comfortable speaking with a woman, I can get my partner, Officer Maynard."

"No, it's okay. Sorry, I just ... No, it's okay."

"You sure?"

She nodded.

"Okay. Can you tell me what happened? What's the first thing you remember?"

"I remember waking up. It was dark. I couldn't see anything. I couldn't move."

"He kept you restrained? The nurses didn't note any restraint marks on your ankles or wrists."

"He kept me in a mattress."

His gaze shot over his notepad. "I'm sorry?"

"A mattress. He'd cut part of it out. He laid me in it, then stitched it shut. When he wanted me, he would cut me out of it, but he always put me back."

"Wait. So, you couldn't move around? You couldn't walk,

or sit up, anything like that?"

"Not unless he was there."

From her place beside the bed, Nancy interjected. "Initial examination shows signs of muscle deterioration. It's likely she had little to no physical activity during her captivity. Except ..." She caught herself, turned hurriedly back to her work.

"The sex."

Nancy's gaze met Kelly's, a mixture of compassion and sorrow marring her features. She nodded. "Yes. Of that, I'm very sorry to say, there was plenty."

"So, he raped you?"

Officer Franko's words brought her head back around.

"Yes."

"More than once?"

"Every day."

His hand stilled above his notepad. His gaze shot to hers.

"Every day?"

"Yes."

"You're sure?"

Incredulity swamped her. For a moment, she could only stare at him, eyes wide, brows drawn, mouth slightly ajar. *Is he serious?*

"Am I sure? *Am I sure?* Yes, you inconsiderate asshole, I'm sure. Every day, he pulled me out of that mattress, carried me over to a bed across the room, spread me out, and fucked me. If I struggled, he drugged me. But first he would beat me into submission. He would beat me, then drug me, then rape me. Then he would cry and apologize and beg for forgiveness before he carried me back across the room, laid me in that godforsaken mattress, and stitched me up. You wanna know how I finally got away? I blew him. I pretended to like it. I told him I loved him. I let him fuck my mouth until he came so hard he nearly passed out from it, and then I shot him up with his own drugs. And now, if you don't mind, yes, I think

I'd be more comfortable with your partner."

Heavy silence fell when she finished.

Finally, "Kelly, I'm so sorry, I didn't mean ..."

"Go to hell."

"You should probably go now." Nancy crossed to Officer Franko, took his arm, and escorted him out of the room. Her disgust was obvious.

When she returned, she gathered up her equipment, along with the specimens she'd gathered. "I'll be back shortly. I'm going to go drop these off at the lab, then get your medication in case of certain STI's. Is there anything else I can bring you?"

"No. I'm fine."

It was the second biggest lie she'd told in her life.

The next six months were hell on earth.

Nothing came of the rape kit. Whoever her attacker was, he wasn't in the system. No one recognized his sketch—brought to life by her memories—plastered all over the city. The police had no new leads; nothing to offer but their apologies and the empty assurances they'd keep looking.

She met weekly with a psychiatrist. According to the woman, she was suffering from PTSD and showed signs of depression and clinical anxiety. *Gee, you think?* Week after week the woman repeated the same annoying mantra: Just give it time, you will heal. Apparently, six months wasn't enough.

The medications did nothing but make her sleepy, so she quit taking them; sleep was something she did her best to avoid.

When John heard she'd been found—not that she'd ever technically been lost—he rushed over to see her. Kelly was happy to see him, she really was. But no matter how hard she tried, she couldn't get past everything that had happened. The first time he pulled her into an embrace, she flew into a panic. He wasn't concerned. Not initially. They'd just take it slow, go at her pace. Things would be fine.

After a couple weeks, he started asking her questions. It would help to talk about it, he said. He sounded like her shrink. He would though, wouldn't he? He had a master's in psychology, after all. When she couldn't bear to hear him badger her anymore, she let him know exactly what happened. She described things in great detail, especially that last day, when she'd imagined it was his cock she was sucking so she could get away. Was that what he wanted to hear? Was that what he needed to know? That a stranger had fucked her so much he'd ruined her for other men. That every ounce of her trust in men had been completely disintegrated. That John might never be able to physically touch her again without her cringing. That the monster who'd raped her had weaseled his way into their relationship, and she'd never be able to look at John without seeing *him*. Had he heard enough? Did he feel helped?

She hadn't seen him since that day. She should have cared.

She didn't tell anyone about the baby. Her trip to the clinic was nearly as traumatic as the three months of captivity had been. She wept through the entire procedure. She wept for the pain. She wept for herself. Most of all, she wept for the baby she wanted to love but was doomed to hate.

Afterwards, she sank deeper and deeper into despondency. She didn't eat. She slept because she could no longer stay awake, only to be assaulted by nightmares that left her screaming in terror. She said less and less at her psychiatrist appointments, preferring to remain silent and withdrawn.

Nothing could bring Kelly out of her spiral. Her mother tried desperately to engage her; she offered to take her out, encouraged her to find a support group, and even suggested she return to school. She might as well have said nothing, for all the good it did.

Kelly had ceased to live. She merely existed.

Kelly drifted aimlessly into the kitchen. She wasn't sure

why, as she had no intention of eating, but it was routine: get out of bed, quick stop at the bathroom, head to the kitchen. Her mother was usually there. Today, however, the kitchen was empty.

She walked to the refrigerator, opened it. Stared inside. Saw nothing. Closed it. She almost missed the note hanging from the Rogers Dental magnet.

Hey honey, hope you're doing okay this morning. Sorry I missed you. Had to leave early for a work meeting. Won't have time to hit the store today. Left $20 on the counter. Will you walk over to Lowry's and pick up a pizza for dinner? Maybe a salad? Thanks, sweetie! Love you, Mom.

Dammit! She didn't want to go to the store. She just wanted to curl up on the couch and zone out to reruns of *America's Next Top Model.* Her mom didn't ask for much, though, and it was only three blocks away. Ten minutes, fifteen tops, and she could be back in her pajamas. Maybe she'd pick up a pint of mint chocolate chip ice cream, too. She'd see.

She trudged upstairs, threw on a pair of jeans and a ratty St. Louis Zoo t-shirt. Both hung away from her body, swallowing her emaciated form. She barely noticed. Sliding her feet into a pair of flip-flops, she headed back downstairs, grabbed the twenty, and walked out the door.

She traversed the three blocks quickly, and sooner than she'd have liked, she found herself outside the local grocery mart. With a bracing inhale, she stepped inside, dreading the assault of other people on her senses.

The noise was loud, brassy. She inwardly cringed. The lights seemed overly bright, stinging her eyes. The scent of fresh fruit rose up to tickle her nostrils; she fought the urge to vomit. She wanted to run. To get away. To escape. She turned, prepared to race the three blocks home, when something stopped her.

"Thanks for shopping at Lowry's, have a good day, sir."

A chill skittered down her spine. *That voice.* She knew that voice. Woodenly, she turned, searching for the sound.

"Hello, ma'am, how are you today?"

There. The checkout line. Swiping groceries in plain sight. Three blocks from her fucking house. As if nothing ever happened. As if he hadn't stolen three months of her life—nine actually, if she included the last six months she'd spent living like a zombie. As if he hadn't utterly destroyed her.

He was different. No longer blonde, he'd dyed his hair. Brown. Grown it out, too. To his shoulders. The facial hair was new, as well.

And then, realization dawned. She knew him. It wasn't just that she recognized him. She knew who he was. *Dylan Rawles.* He'd rung up and bagged her groceries more times than she could count. Every time she came through his line, he said hello, called her by name. They shared small talk. He would smile at her, sometimes slip a chocolate bar into her bag if his boss wasn't looking. Once he'd even suggested they catch a movie sometime. She'd responded vaguely, saying something like, "Yeah, maybe."

Her stomach roiled. He'd asked her that not too long before he abducted her. Had he taken her ambiguous answer as an affirmative? Had that slim possibility been to him an absolute? Yes. What had been a polite brush-off on her part, he'd taken as a declaration of returned affection. And permission to hold her hostage, apparently.

The sudden surge of anger shocked her. Whenever she'd imagined facing her abductor—and her dreams made sure she did—she'd always melted into a quivering puddle of panic. She could never run fast enough, and her cries for help went unanswered. She always ended up back in the mattress, her lungs locked in a never-ending scream.

Except now she stood here, and there he was, less than ten yards away, working a stone's throw away from her home. It wasn't enough, what he'd done to her. Still, he invaded her space, threatened her person. Was he stalking her now? Just waiting for her to emerge from her solitude, waiting for the chance to take her again? Waiting to renew their "love?"

The fear she should have felt didn't stand a chance against the disgusted rage that spurred her into action. Heading down the frozen food aisle, she pulled a pepperoni pizza out, along with the ice cream she now suddenly craved. Tossing them in her basket, she walked over to the fresh produce, grabbed some lettuce, a tomato, cucumber, and green pepper. She hoped there was some kind of dressing at the house.

Then, she got in line.

He hadn't noticed her yet. Setting the basket at her feet, she gathered the extra cloth of her t-shirt, tied it in a knot at her back, exposing her midriff. She ran her hands through her hair, giving it a tousled and — hopefully — sexy look. There was nothing she could do about the baggy jeans, but the loose fit did show more skin. It would have to be enough. For now.

"Thanks, Mrs. Knight, have a great day!"

It was her turn. She set her basket on the conveyer belt, watched it roll toward him. Waving to the old lady walking out the door, he turned and reached for her basket, not falling out of his work rhythm.

"Thanks for choosing Lowry's, how are you today?"

"I'm good, Dylan, how are you?"

He jerked; his eyes shot to her, and his shock was evident. It was quickly and smoothly concealed, however, replaced by an easy, pleased smile.

"Kelly! It's been a while. I haven't seen you in what? Six, seven months?"

"Something like that. I was gone for a while."

He nodded in concern, reached out to touch her shoulder. "I heard about what happened. I'm so sorry. How are you holding up?"

"I'm managing. It's been rough, but I think I'm finally ready to start getting back to my life."

"That's good. I can't imagine what it was like."

"I doubt anyone can."

"That's true." He swiped the pizza, the ice cream, the vegetables, bagged them carefully. "Well, I'm glad you're doing alright. I got pretty worried when I didn't see you for so long. That'll be $18.34."

She handed him the twenty. His fingers brushed hers; she saw the glint of desire pop in his eyes. He opened the drawer, slid the bill in, pulled her change.

"There you are, Kelly. Don't be a stranger."

"I won't. Thanks, Dylan. It's good to know I've got people around who care — people like you." She brushed his arm lightly. His smile bloomed.

"Have a good day, Kelly. I'll see you around."

She smiled and waved as she slipped out the door. *Yes, Dylan. You most certainly will.*

She didn't sleep that night. A whirlwind of emotion whipped through her. *Why has he left me alone?* Surely, he knew she was back home. He worked three blocks away, for God's sake. And he was obviously unduly aware of her; he had been for months. Pacing furiously across her floor, she made a mental list of everything she knew about Dylan Rawles.

He was a perfectly average person. Six-foot. Blonde. Thin, but not skinny. Fit, but not overly muscular. He wasn't bad looking, though she wouldn't categorize him as more than mildly attractive. Despite being friendly, he was always a bit awkward. And while he did well at Lowry's, it seemed evident to her he'd never rise much higher than an outstanding grocery clerk. He was the type of person who knew he was average, and was content to be so.

Or so she'd thought.

He'd been flirting with her for months, she realized. She'd always thought he was just being nice, but no. To him, it had been flirting. And somehow, he'd deluded himself into thinking his feelings for her were mutual.

What had she done to make him think that? Had she flirted back? She didn't think so; he'd been friendly, and she'd responded in kind. And what about John? Surely he'd known about her boyfriend, so why? Why would Dylan think she had feelings for him?

Because he's crazy.

A barrage of memories overtook her. She remembered in excruciating detail every time he'd told he loved her — sincerity tinged with desperation. He believed it, and he needed her to believe it, too. Every time he'd pushed inside her. Gentle determination. He didn't want to hurt her, but he was going to have her. Every time he'd orgasmed. His breath hitched, he shuddered, then collapsed on top of her and nuzzled her neck.

A shiver crawled down her spine, followed by a warming heat. Her breath quickened. Red tinged her peripheral vision. The rage came suddenly, flowing over her, embracing her, driving away the fear, the depression, the perplexity.

That lousy sonofabitch!

He'd taken everything from her! He'd destroyed her! Where once she'd been a beautiful, lively, outgoing nursing student with everything to live for, she was now a hollowed-out shell that spurned connection, intent on existing in isolation. She'd driven John away, ignored her friends, shut out her mother, given up on herself.

Killed a child.

Angry sobs ripped out of her chest. *God, how I hate him!* Whirling around, she grabbed the closest thing to her — her copy of *Pride and Prejudice*. She hurled it at the wall. The lamp followed, the bulb shattering. Then her alarm clock, a glass paperweight, her anatomy textbook.

"I hate you! I hate you, I hate you, I HATE YOU!"

"Kelly? Kelly, what's going on?!" Her mother rushed into

the room, grabbing hold of her arms. "Kelly!"

Kelly collapsed against her, continuing to weep. "I'm sorry, Mom. So sorry."

"Shh, it's okay. You don't need to be sorry."

"I'm sorry. I hate him, Mom. I hate him so much."

"I know, sweetie. I know."

Her mom held and rocked her for long minutes, until her sobs finally subsided. Pulling free, she wiped the residual tears from her cheeks, rubbed her eyes.

"I'm sorry, Mom. I didn't mean to wake you. I wasn't thinking."

"Kelly, you don't have to apologize."

"I know, I just … I shouldn't have woken you."

"Sweetie, it's okay. I'm glad I woke up. Frankly, I'm relieved. You've been so withdrawn, so … apathetic. I've been so worried about you. You needed to let everything out. I wanted to help you let everything out, but I just didn't know how. I've felt so useless."

"No, Mom, it wasn't your fault."

"It wasn't yours, either. You know that, right?"

She did. Now.

"He needs to pay, Mom."

"Aww, sweetie, I know. For every second of hell he put you through. And he will, I'm sure of it. Someday, somehow, he will."

Kelly nodded, then reached out to hug her mother. "I love you, Mom."

"I love you, too, baby. Try and get some sleep, okay?" Donna hesitated for a moment, then went on. "It's good to have you back."

"'Night, Mom."

"Goodnight, Kelly."

She watched her mom close the door behind her, then turned to clean up the mess she'd made. All cried out, the despair and anguish had drained away. All that remained was the hatred, and it had cooled. She was calm now, collected. And she had a feeling her mother's "someday, somehow" would be coming a lot sooner than either of them expected.

Dylan stared at her across the booth. Their waiter had taken their plates, surreptitiously slid the check onto the corner of the table, and left them to linger over cups of coffee. Throughout dinner, they'd engaged in small talk and chitchat, avoiding anything heavy. She inquired about his position at Lowry's. He was managing now. He asked if she planned to go back to school. She said she wasn't sure yet if a career in nursing was for her; she thought she might be happy being a wife and mother—when that time came, of course. His eyes glinted at that.

The reprieve was over, though. His mood was starting to darken; she knew why. She also knew what she had to do. If things were going to progress—if she was going to succeed—she had to convince him she'd seen the error of her ways. More, that she was willing to accept any punishment he thought necessary. She knew enough of him to be certain; he wasn't planning on letting her get away with her escape unscathed.

She glanced down at her coffee, ran her finger around the rim of the cup, looked up at him shyly, then looked back down.

"I'm sorry, Dylan."

He didn't answer. Just continued to stare.

"I shouldn't have hurt you. Shouldn't have left."

"No. You shouldn't have."

She looked back up. He was angrier than she'd first suspected. She could sense his temper, simmering beneath a calm facade. He was struggling to keep it leashed. For a split second, the scene changed. They were back in that basement, and he backhanded her, splitting her lip. She winced.

"Please try to understand, Dylan. I was scared."

"Of what? *Of me?* There's no reason for you to be scared of me, Kelly. I love you. I would do anything for you. You know that."

"I do. I do know. I meant I was scared of myself. Of the strength of my feelings for you. I've never felt about anyone the way I feel about you." *Isn't that the truth?*

"And how do you feel?"

She took a deep breath. *This is it.* "I love you, Dylan. So much. You took such good care of me, loved me so well. I didn't deserve it. I don't deserve it. I don't deserve you. I was worried you would grow tired of me, worried you would break my heart. That's why I left."

"How could you think that? I could never grow tired of you! You're everything to me, Kelly. Everything!"

His voice lifted. The couple at the next booth glanced over at them, eyebrows raised. She reached out to calm him, gripping his hand across the table.

"I was wrong. I know that now. But …" She trailed off. Her lip trembled. Her eyes watered. "You didn't come after me."

"How could I? You tricked me with sex, then ran away from me. I thought it was pretty clear you didn't want me anymore. And I could never purposely do anything to make you unhappy."

"But I do want you, Dylan. That's why I came back. When you didn't come after me, I thought it was over. We were over. But I've been miserable. I haven't been able to sleep, haven't been able to eat. I couldn't do it anymore. I had to know. I had to see if we could go back to what we were. I had to see if you could ever forgive me. Can you, Dylan? Can you forgive me?"

He was dying to say yes; she could see it. But she knew he wouldn't let a chance to punish her go by. He never could. *Manipulative bastard.*

She slid out of her side of the booth, slipped in close beside him. She looked up at him imploringly, let her hand fall gently on his knee. "Please, Dylan. Please say you'll forgive me." And then she lifted her lips to his.

He resisted, but only for a moment. Then his fingers tangled in her hair, and he dragged her closer. Deepened the kiss. She threw herself into it, letting him hold her, caress her. Before, she could have never allowed his touch; now, everything was in pursuit of her ultimate goal.

Screw justice.

Vengeance would be sweeter.

She opened her mouth to accept his tongue, sucked on it, heard him moan. Her lips curved in a smile. He might be angry with her, but he wanted her, too. His desire was a rope, and she had every intention of hanging him with it.

She pulled away, settled her head on his shoulder, cuddled in close. "Is that a yes?"

He ran a finger up and down her cheek, sighed heavily. "I forgive you, Kelly."

She smiled, then gasped when he gripped her chin, yanked her head up to face him. "But you have to promise you'll never leave me again. I won't stand for it, Kelly. I can't live without you, and I won't allow you to live without me. Understand?"

"I understand."

"That's not enough. Say it, Kelly. Promise me."

"I will never leave you again, Dylan. I promise."

Over the next month, she saw Dylan nearly every day. She dropped in on him at work. They went out to dinner, or the movies. She even introduced him to her mother.

They kissed in the restaurants, necked in the theatres, made out in his car. But it never went any farther than that. She would die before she'd let him inside her again — not that she had any intention of telling him that. Rather, she led him on.

"Not yet, Dylan. We're getting to know each other all over again. This is our new start. And our first time should be special."

"It will be special, Kelly. Because it's us."

"I know. But when you make love to me, I want to be sure there aren't any doubts left between us. I want you to know you can trust me. Completely. Please be patient just a little longer. Please?"

He'd shaken his head, grinned, and then kissed her. He hadn't pressed her since then, but he was losing his patience.

That was fine. She was more than ready — she had been since she'd started this farce — and she was pretty sure she'd convinced him. She would find out soon. Right or wrong, it didn't matter. One of them would be dead, and this ordeal would be over.

She took extra care with her appearance that evening. She spent a long time in the shower, conditioning her hair twice, shaving every inch of her legs and underarms, using scented bath oil instead of body wash. She dried, then curled her hair, letting it fall in loose waves down her back. She applied her makeup meticulously. Her eyes became dark and seductive, her lips luscious. Next came the lacy black thong, followed by the short, strapless, black number she'd bought specifically for this night. She didn't bother with a bra. Finally, she pulled out a pair of black, thigh-high, heeled leather boots. She'd paid a fortune for them, with a little extra for the custom concealed holster inside the right, but it was worth it. Tonight was going to be memorable, after all.

Grabbing her clutch, she slipped into her mom's bedroom, punched in the code on the safe, and withdrew the S&W .357 Magnum. She popped the cylinder, loaded the six chambers, snapped it shut. The Lady Smith model was a bit smaller than most, designed specifically by Smith and Wesson for a female's grip; it fit Kelly's palm like the handshake of an old friend. When Kelly's father had died ten years ago, Donna had bought the revolver, and she'd insisted that she and Kelly both learn how to shoot it. And shoot it well. Kelly had spent her fair share of time at the range, and her aim was pretty damn good, if she did say so herself.

She slid the gun into the holster of her boot. The metal was cool and comforting against her thigh. Pulling the hem of her dress down over the top of the boots, she checked to make sure the revolver wasn't noticeable. Then, locking the safe back up, she headed down the stairs.

Her mom was in the kitchen, boiling some spaghetti. Kelly tapped her on the shoulder, gave a little twirl.

"Wow. Aren't you a sight this evening? Special occasion?"

Very special. "Not really. Just felt like getting all dolled up."

"Well, you certainly succeeded. Dylan's going to swallow his tongue."

Not quite. I've got something better planned.

Kelly laughed. "I hope not. That would make certain … things … difficult."

That caught her mom off-guard. "Oh. You think it's going that far?"

"Maybe. Maybe not. I don't know for sure yet. Why? Do you not like him, Mom?"

"Oh, no, sweetie, it's not that. I just … It hasn't been that long since … I just don't want to see you get hurt."

Kelly reached out and hugged her mom. "Don't worry, Mom. I'm okay, really." *That bastard's never going to hurt me again.*

"Really?" Her mom pulled her away, looked at her hard.

"Really. Promise."

The doorbell drew both their attention. "That'll be Dylan."

"Have a wonderful time. I love you, Kelly."

"I love you, too, Mom. Don't wait up, okay?"

"Okay. Just be safe, alright?"

"You can count on that."

He didn't quite swallow his tongue, but it was close. His response was immediate; she noticed the telltale twitch behind his fly. She gave him a satisfied smile.

"Hey, baby. Like it?"

"I don't think 'like' even begins to cover it."

"Good. That was the goal." She leaned in to press a quick peck against his cheek. "So where are we going?"

"Well, I thought we might grab dinner at the Spaghetti Factory, then maybe take a carriage ride through downtown, but this get-up you're in seems like it might be wasted on that."

She slipped her arm into his as they headed for the car, pressed up against him. "Well, in all honesty, I'm not that hungry. Not for food anyway." And then she gazed up at him, letting her eyes say everything else.

His eyes widened. "Yeah? You mean …?"

"Mm-hmm." She slid past the passenger door he held for her, settled into the seat. When he got in beside her, he was still stammering.

"Wow, um, okay. Yeah, wow. Alright."

"So that's a yes?"

"Abso-fucking-lutely! Shit, sorry, that was crude."

"Not at all. I know I've made you wait, and I want you to know how much I really appreciate it." She let her hand slip between his legs, rubbed against his erection.

He groaned, lifted his hips. "Shit, Kelly." And then he was on top of her, pressing her back in her seat, his lips ravaging hers, his hands fighting to get under her dress.

She burst into laughter. He pulled back, looked at her incredulously.

"What?"

"In the car, Dylan? Really?"

"What do you want from me? I'm just a man, Kelly."

You wish, fucker.

"I'm sorry, I shouldn't have teased so much. But tonight needs to be special. Slow. Savored." She flicked her tongue against her lower lip, ran it up and around her upper lip. She then leaned in and kissed him slowly. "I want you to make

70

love to me, Dylan. All night. I don't want just a quick screw in your backseat. Especially not in view of my mother's living room." She indicated they were still sitting in the driveway of her house.

"Shit. You're right, of course. Sorry. So, where did you have in mind?" He started the car, put it in gear.

"I think you know."

His gaze shot to hers.

"Take me back, Dylan. To where you first made love to me. Take me home."

His breath hitched. His eyes glazed over just a bit. Then, with a slight shake, his hands tightened on the wheel, his foot slammed on the gas, and they shot off into the darkening evening.

He parked in front of a small house on The Hill. One story, red bricked, with patches of marigolds popping from planters beneath the front windows. It was quaint and charming, in direct contrast to the horror she'd suffered within.

"It's beautiful, Dylan." That much was true. "Is it yours?"

"My mother's. She died about a year ago. I've kept it up since then."

"I'm sorry. Were you close?"

"We were. Until the end." He slid out of the car, came around to open her door.

"What happened?" She took his offered hand, stepped out beside him.

He shrugged. "Let's just say, she didn't quite … understand … the direction my life was headed in. She didn't exactly approve."

Cryptic. Was he referring to his dead-end job? Or to her? *About a year ago …* That would have been not too long before he'd abducted her. How convenient his mother had left him a perfect place to stage her captivity. A sense of dread descended over her. Still, she kept her tone light.

"How did she die? Was she sick?"

71

"No. There … There was a … an accident." He wouldn't meet her eyes, and suddenly there was no doubt in her mind. He'd engineered his mother's death. Murdered her, so he could take Kelly. The sonofabitch really was insane.

"I'm sorry, I shouldn't have asked. I'm sure it hurts to talk about it."

He nodded. "Yeah …"

"Well, let's not think about it." She leaned up, kissed his cheek. "Take me inside, Dylan. We've got better things to do than dwell on the dead."

He perked up at that. His eyes darkened, and his head swooped down to take her lips in a hard, fast kiss. "You're right about that."

They stepped onto the porch. He pulled a key from above the doorframe, unlocked the door. Slipping the key back in its hiding spot, he pulled her inside, shut the door behind them.

"Do you want the tour now or later?"

"Later, definitely later. There's only one room I want to see right now."

He grinned, then led her down a hallway that split the house in half. About a third of the way down was a door. He paused in front of it, opened it, gestured for her to head down the stairs. They were unfinished, with a wall on either side about halfway down; then they opened to either side, with no bannister. She stepped carefully, and kept a firm grip on Dylan's hand as she descended.

When she reached the bottom, she let go of him and slowly spun around. Memories assaulted her, rushing back over her in a furious wave. There, below the high, six-inch window was the bed where he'd raped her. Every day. For three months. It was covered in the same plain, black sheets she remembered. And there was the door to the bathroom; those few moments alone and free each day had been her only solace. And there, only a few yards away, was the mattress where he'd kept her.

It was in the same basic metal frame, with no head or

footboard. A thick comforter covered it, along with a pile of pillows. She'd seen them piled beside the mattress a number of times when he pulled her from it. A simple deception, in case anyone managed to make it down here; it looked like a regular bed, if a bit unornate. She knew better. Below that comforter was the three-foot split that he'd sewn and ripped apart and sewn, again and again. *Did he bother to stitch it shut after I escaped?*

He walked past her, heading for the other bed. "How about I turn the sheets down?"

"I don't think so, asshole."

He turned at the venom in her tone, his eyes widening as he noticed the Magnum she'd slipped from her holster, and now had pointed directly at his heart. He smiled slightly, raised his hands up in front of his chest.

"What is this, Kelly?"

She didn't answer; her grip tightened on the gun. He smirked, took a step toward her.

"I wouldn't do that, Dylan, if I were you."

"Why? You going to kill me?"

"Yes."

He pulled up for just a moment. Then he snickered. "C'mon, Kelly. You're not going to shoot me." Obviously unperturbed by the weapon in her hands, he took another step. She adjusted her aim, pulled the trigger.

The blast cracked in her ears, ricocheted off the concrete walls.

"You bitch!" Screaming, Dylan crumpled to the floor before her, blood pouring from a hole just below his knee. He stared at it for a moment, uncomprehending, then glared up at her, his eyes hot with rage. Holding his knee to try and staunch the bleeding, he lurched to his feet, panting in pain, and started to lunge forward. Her next bullet embedded itself in the carpet a mere inch from his toes. He halted. Fury and caution warred on his features. And then his mask was back in place. Sorrow, hurt, betrayal all shone from his face. His eyes brimmed with tears.

"Why are you doing this, Kelly?"

"Shut up, Dylan."

"I thought we meant something to each other!"

"You're delusional."

He looked up, studied her for a moment. Apparently deciding that tactic wasn't going to work, he tried another. Clutching his leg, he hunched in on himself, and his voice took on a whiny, piteous tone.

"Kelly, my leg hurts. It hurts bad. I'm bleeding all over the place. I need to go to the hospital. Please, you have to call an ambulance."

"Not yet." Readjusting, she lifted the gun to point once again at his chest.

Panic took over then, and he cried, pleading with her. "Kelly, don't do this. Please, don't kill me. I'm sorry. I'm sorry if I hurt you, I tried so hard to be gentle. I never wanted to hurt you, I love you, Kelly, do you hear me? I love you. I've always loved you. You can't do this! Please don't do this! It wasn't my fault! It wasn't my fault you were so beautiful, and you led me on, you did! You made me believe you loved me. That's why I brought you here, because you loved me, and I loved you. We're supposed to be together, Kelly. Forever! Don't do this, please, I'm begging you!"

She let him rant, let him beg and plead. Angry tears brimmed as she stared at him with blatant hate and undeserved pity. And then she squeezed the trigger.

The resulting silence was deafening. She watched the blood pool in a puddle beneath his crumpled body. His eyes were still open, wide with fear and an absurd level of hope. She waited for a sense of relief, a sense of finality to descend.

Time drifted while she stood there. She didn't know how much had passed before she finally gave herself a mental shake; the plan wasn't quite finished. Not yet.

Reaching into her clutch, she pulled out her phone, brought up the list of contacts. She'd programmed Officer Franko's number in, at her mother's insistence. Not that she'd ever bothered to call the sexist asshole. *Am I sure? Jackass.* But he would come in handy now.

She took a deep breath, let the tears finally fall. They weren't sad tears, but they would do the job. Then she hit "call." Lifting the phone to her ear, she listened to it ring. Once. Twice. On the third ring, a male voice answered.

"Officer Franko."

"Hi. Officer Franko? This is ... Oh, God, this is Kelly Johnson. I ... I shot him."

"I'm sorry?"

"I shot him!"

"Kelly, what are you talking about? Shot who?"

"Dylan, I shot Dylan!"

"Who's Dylan?"

"My boyfriend. Except, he ... He isn't my boyfriend, he's ... He's my rapist."

"Wait, Kelly, back up for a minute. You shot your boyfriend?"

"Yes! Except no. I didn't know who he really was. I shot him, Officer Franko, I ... I think ... I think he's dead."

"Okay, Kelly, where are you?"

She gave him the address.

"Okay, just stay there. Can you do that?"

"Uh-huh."

"Good. I'm going to send a unit out, and I am on my way. I'll be there soon. Just stay calm, okay?"

"I'll ... I'll try. Please hurry."

He hung up, and she smiled through the tears when she heard the dial tone. *Take your time, Officer.* She glanced back at the heap on the floor. *He's not coming back.*

The cops believed her story. It wasn't hard to convince them, all things considered. She hadn't recognized Dylan Rawles as her rapist when she'd run across him at the grocery market. He'd disguised himself, after all. She remembered him as someone she saw in passing, someone she'd never really noticed before the abduction. But he was so nice to her that day she'd stopped in for a pizza, asking if she was okay, if there was anything he could do to help her. They'd talked a few times after that, and when he'd asked her out to dinner, it seemed natural to say yes.

"He was so nice, such a gentleman. Always bringing me flowers or dropping by with a bag of cherry slices from the store. He knew they were my favorite."

Kelly sat, shoulders hunched, her arms wrapped around her middle. Officer Franko had taken the gun as soon as he arrived and handed it off to one of his partners. Kelly didn't object.

"So, you saw him often?"

"Yes, we started seeing each other regularly. Two or three times a week. He was so perfect, so ..." She trailed off with a shrug, letting her eyes fill with tears.

"And you never suspected him? Never recognized him?"

"No. It seems crazy, I know, but I didn't. Neither did my mother, and she'll tell you she's an excellent judge of character. He fooled us both. Completely."

Officer Franko nodded, taking notes in a small flipbook.

"So, what happened tonight?"

"Dylan told me he wanted to take me somewhere special tonight. He didn't tell me where, just said it was going to be a night to remember. I was so excited, so full of anticipation. I even went out and bought a new dress, new boots." She gestured toward her outfit.

"It's a very lovely outfit, Kelly."

"Thanks. I'll never wear it again. Not now. I just want to take it off and get rid of it." She fidgeted restlessly, emphasizing her words.

"That's understandable. What happened next?"

"He drove us out to The Hill. When I realized where he was headed, I was sure he was taking me to one of the Italian restaurants. Trattoria Marcella, or something like that. But instead, he pulled up here, in front of this house. I got a little worried. What with my history and all, I'll admit I was nervous. But then he told me it was his mother's.

"'You're going to introduce me to your mother?' I said. 'Why didn't you tell me?' Now I was really nervous, but in a completely different way. I was so worried about my dress, that she would think it was too much, too slutty. I should have brought her some wine, or at least some flowers. I was completely unprepared!

"He just laughed at me. He swore his mother would think I was perfect, then gave me a reassuring kiss. He knocked then, but nobody answered."

Officer Franko glanced up. "She wasn't home?"

"Dylan said she was. He used the spare key to let us in, and when we walked into the foyer, we could hear water running. He said she probably lost track of time and was still in the shower. He offered to give me a tour while we were waiting."

"So you never saw Mrs. Rawles?"

Kelly shook her head. One of the other officers came up behind Franko and leaned down to murmur in his ear. A moment later, the other officer walked away, and Franko looked up at Kelly.

"It turns out Dylan Rawles' mother died about a year ago in some sort of freak accident."

Yeah, a freak accident called murder. She held the snide comment in, and let shock flood her features; she hoped it rang true.

"That's so horrible!"

"We'll be looking into it. Could be, given the circumstanc-

77

es, her so-called accident might have been something else.

Well, lookie here, everybody. Officer Franko has a brain.

"So, once you were inside, what happened then?"

"He told me he wanted to show me the basement first. He said he had a workshop down there, and wanted to show it to me. We went down the stairs, and that's when I saw the mattress. And then I knew. I realized everything was a lie. But I couldn't believe it. I didn't want to believe it. I knew what my attacker looked like; I'd seen him every day for three months. It couldn't be Dylan!" She stopped for a moment; a few quiet sobs tore their way free. When she looked up at Officer Franko, tears were streaming down her face. "He was so perfect. So kind and generous and loving. How could he fool me like that? Why didn't I see it? Why didn't I recognize him? I should have recognized him!"

She continued to sob as Franko reached over to lay a hand on her shoulder. "Serial rapists are manipulators, Kelly. That's what they do, how they work. They study their victims and prey on their vulnerabilities. Don't beat yourself up over it; you have nothing to feel bad or guilty about. This is on him, not you. Do you hear me?"

Kelly managed to nod and swiped her knuckled beneath her eyes.

"Good. Can you go on?"

"Yes."

"Okay. So you saw the mattress, realized who he was. Then what?"

"That's when I pulled the gun."

"I understand the situation, Kelly, so I'm very sorry, but I have to ask about that. Does the gun belong to you?"

"No. Yes. Well, kind of."

"Can you clarify that?"

"My mother originally bought the gun."

"Is it registered?"

"Yes. When I turned twenty-one, she went with me, and I

registered it as well. Basically, we have dual ownership of it."

"Okay. Do you have a FOID card? Permit?"

"Yes and yes. I have them with me if you'd like to see them."

"I do need to see them, yes."

Kelly dipped her head and reached for her purse. Pulling out a small wallet, she dug out the cards and handed them over. After a quick but careful perusal, Officer Franko handed them back.

"Any reason you had the gun on you tonight?"

"After the abduction, I started carrying it regularly. Even in the house, I didn't like to be without it. I was so scared he was going to come after me again, and I wasn't going back."

"Did you usually carry it with you when you were out with Dylan?"

"Yes. I carried it with me whenever I went out; it didn't matter where I was going or who I was with."

"Did Dylan know?"

"No. I mentioned it once, and he told me he didn't much care for firearms. It wasn't an argument I wanted to have, so I kept the information to myself."

"Do you know how to shoot it?" Franko's stared directly at her, his question frank.

"Yes. My mother made sure of that. I never thought I would actually have to, though."

"We never do."

They sat silently for a moment, both pondering. Then Franko asked her to continue.

"I just wanted him to let me go. I told him if he let me go and never bothered me again, I wouldn't say anything. I wouldn't turn him in. He could just go on with his life, as long as he left me out of it. But he wouldn't agree to that. He swore he would never let me go again. That I was his, that we belonged together. And then he started to come towards me.

"I fired a warning shot into the floor, hoping he'd realize

I was serious. 'I don't want to shoot you,' I told him. But he wouldn't listen. He didn't stop. So I shot him in the knee. He went down, hard. I thought maybe then he'd let me go, but I'd just made him mad. He started yelling at me, screaming and cursing, and then he lunged at me. He was going to kill me. I knew it. I knew that if he got to me, he would kill me. He was that angry. So I shot him in the chest."

She looked down at the floor, then up at Officer Franko. "I didn't want to kill him. You have to believe me. I'm so, so sorry. I just wanted him to let me go. I just wanted the nightmare to be over. I'm sorry. I'm sorry I killed him, I didn't want to. I swear. I'm sorry!"

She collapsed into a fit of hysterical tears, repeating "I'm sorry" over and over again. Officer Franko came to sit next to her, wrapped an arm around her shoulders, and tried to quiet her, assuring her everything was going to be all right.

Finally, with a series of hiccups, she calmed. "I want to go home. Can I? Go home? Please? Is this over?"

It was over. Officer Franko assured her it was an open-and-shut case. The proper paperwork would be filled out. No charges would be pressed. This was an obvious case of self-defense. And yes, he'd be happy to drive her home.

Kelly was walking across the quad of Washington University when she saw him. She came to a halt, her heart pounding. He was tall, blonde, his profile hinting at fine features. Her vision wavered. No. It wasn't Dylan. Dylan was dead. She'd shot him.

But this guy. He looked so much like him. *And look.* Just look at the way he was looking at that girl he was talking to.

Predatory. Like a big cat hunting its next meal. Just like *he* had hunted her. This guy, he was like Dylan—just a different side to the same coin. She knew it. She could feel it in every quivering inch of her body. She couldn't let him hurt that girl.

She wouldn't let him get away with it!

Sliding against the thick trunk of a tree, she watched him. Images of a certain basement, a certain mattress swam in front of her eyes. The house on The Hill was hers now. When the city put it up for auction, she'd won it for a measly five grand; no one wanted the house of a known rapist and murderer, no matter how premium the property. She had no plans for it. She only knew she didn't want it being used again. Ever.

Watching this slimy bastard, however, she realized that had been a mistake. Perhaps that mattress had a greater purpose. Maybe it *should* be used again. No one would miss this guy. No one missed Dylan, after all. And one less sexual predator on the loose could only be a good thing. They would learn. Sewn up in that mattress, these bastards would learn to leave women like her alone.

When the girl walked away, he watched her—and Kelly watched him. And when he finally turned and headed down the street, she slipped from the shadows and followed. Silently, determinedly, the hunted now the hunter. Kelly Johnson stalked her prey.

LUCY

The thunk was normal; the silence that followed was not.

My fingers froze over my keyboard, mid-type. I breathed in, held it. My ears strained as I waited for the tell-tale rush of inhalation followed by a piercing cry. It didn't come.

"Lucy?"

No response.

"Lucy? Are you okay?"

Nothing.

The laptop slid off my knees as I stood, staring toward the stairs. A tightness threatened to settle in my chest. I shook it off. She was fine. Lucy was always fine.

Why wasn't she answering?

"Lucy!"

The steps seemed to rise up and slap against my feet as I climbed the stairs, doing their best to trip me up. The banister, unusually cold against my skin, bit into my palm. A tension that had not been present moments ago permeated the air; the atmosphere within the small apartment reeked of malice.

Stop it. I berated myself for falling prey to my overactive imagination. Our home wasn't out to get me, and there was nothing wrong with my daughter. Hell, Lucy managed to "grievously" injure herself at least twice a day. She was like a battering ram with a head as hard as a bowling ball. My husband, Charlie, and I joked frequently with our friends, Grace and Ronny, about it; on the occasions they'd expressed concern about Lucy running into their marble coffee table, we'd laughed it off, saying they ought to be more worried about the marble cracking than Lucy's head.

My four-year-old was extremely accident prone, it was true, but she never seemed the worse for wear. Always, she popped up with a grin and an immediate "I'm okay," and without another thought, she was at it again. Today would be no different. When I looked into her room, there she'd be, building a tower to the sky and murmuring stories to herself.

She was fine.

So why couldn't I lift the weight of dread from my shoulders?

I stepped onto the landing and turned. Lucy's door was closed. *See?* That's why I didn't hear her respond. Logical explanation.

My fingertips brushed lightly against wood as I swung the bedroom door inward.

"Lucy, honey. You okay?"

I didn't see her at first. Glancing around I noted, with a fair balance of irritation and amusement, the absolute mess that was my daughter's room. Blocks, books, plastic tea cups, princesses, and dinosaurs—they were strewn from one end of the room to other, and every single stuffed animal had been tossed out of the top bunk.

Like always.

"Lucy?"

The scene morphed. Suddenly I was staring at one of the pages of Lucy's favorite optical illusion books; the room appeared empty, just an innocent page covered in lines. But when I tilted my head and crossed my eyes, the illusion disappeared, revealing the hidden dragon with a castle just beyond.

But there was no dragon. No castle. No pleasant image popping into the foreground.

As my gaze scanned the dishevelment, it slowly melted away, fading into the background. My daughter slid into focus.

"Lucy!"

I lunged forward and fell to my knees, the tiled concrete floor unforgiving, frantically tossing toys aside. Panic rose up, a massive wave of uncontrollable anxiety, then crashed over me, leaving me roiling. I was nothing but a mass of clammy skin and overactive nerves.

No. God, no.

"LUCY!"

This isn't happening. This can't be happening. She's fine; she's always fine.

My hands stretched out, grasped her shoulders. I almost shook her.

Stop, you idiot! What are you doing? You can't shake her! Now stop it! Get your shit together. You don't have time to break down now. You have to help your daughter. You have to help Lucy.

My breath shook, fighting, pummeling my throat as I dragged it down into my lungs. Taking my hands away, I let my gaze drift over her, trying to assess the damage. She lay on her back, unconscious. One arm was bent at an unnatural angle—dislocated, at the very least. Blood trickled from her nose. Head trauma. Reaching out, I felt for a pulse. It was there, but I'd forgotten how to count. And the shallow rattle from her lungs…

God, no. Please, no. No.

It seemed like forever until I fumbled with the pocket of my jeans, yanking my phone free. Surely it must have only been a matter of seconds, but time had lost its meaning.

I stared at the screen blankly for a moment. *What …? Oh, right. 911.* I watched, detached, as another's hand held the phone, another's fingers dialed the three simple digits.

"Nine one one, what is your emergency?"

Had I really pushed the speaker button? I must have, as I could hear a reedy voice. What did it say?

"Nine one one. Hello?"

I gripped the phone loosely. It was a wonder I didn't drop it as I stared at the blood on Lucy's face. Was blood always so bright, so garish? Or was it because her face was so pale? So deathly pale…

"… prank calls are taken very seriously. If this is not an emergency, I will be forced to contact the local police and …"

"It's my daughter."

Silence. Then, "I'm sorry?"

"My daughter. She needs help. She's bleeding. I think she's going to die."

The sentences slipped mechanically from my lips. I wasn't sure where the words were coming from. Not from me, surely. The thought of speaking, forming words, exhibiting coherence. I couldn't manage it.

"Ma'am, what is your name? And your address please?"

What was that godawful, nasally sound? And why wouldn't it go away?

"Ma'am, are you there?"

My stomach churned as I looked again at Lucy's arm. Arms weren't supposed to bend that way. What did her arm matter? She wouldn't need it when she was gone. And God would fix it when she was in Heaven, anyway.

"Ma'am? Ma'am! I cannot help you or your daughter if you don't talk to me. I don't want her to die, but if you don't answer me, she could. Do you hear me? She could die. So I need you to answer me! Now, what is your name?"

The no-nonsense, impatient voice was an abrupt slap to the face, dragging me back from the edge of an anxiety attack. Somewhere it registered that she probably wasn't supposed to

yell; it wasn't very professional. Professional or not, though, she'd gotten my attention.

"My name is Susan Roberts. I live at 461 Harrisburg."

There was a sigh on the other end; the huff of breath razed against the speaker of the phone. "Thank you, ma'am. Now, can you tell me what happened?"

"I ... I don't know. I heard a thump upstairs, figured my daughter had tripped or fallen or something. I didn't worry much; she's always doing something or other to herself. She's klutzy, like me. I mean, just last week, I tripped down the stairs and—"

"—Ma'am. I don't mean to be rude, but I need you to stay

on point. You heard a thump. What happened next?"

"Oh, yes, I'm sorry. I heard a thump. I called to my daughter to make sure she was alright. She didn't answer. So I went upstairs to check on her. I found her ... I found her lying on the floor. She won't answer me. She's unconscious. Her right arm is bent at a—God, it's such a horrible angle—and she's bleeding. She's bleeding from her nose."

"How old is she?"

Huh? What the hell did that matter? "She's, uh ... she's four."

"And do you know her approximate weight?"

"Between 35 and 40 pounds."

"Good. Now, does she have a pulse?"

I felt again. The pitter-patter against my fingers was like the brush of a feather. "It's faint."

"Can you count it for me?"

"I'm sorry, I ... I can't ..."

"That's okay, don't worry. But she does have a pulse? You can feel one?"

"Yes."

"Is she breathing?"

"Yes, she's breathing. But it doesn't sound right, though."

"Can you put your phone beside her mouth so I can hear?"

I did. Condensation flared, then dissipated as the screen caught Lucy's ragged breath.

"Alright, good. Thank you, Ms. Roberts. I've already dispatched an ambulance to your location. They should be there shortly."

Very shortly. I could already hear the wail of the siren.

"Now listen to me. I want you to go downstairs and meet the paramedics at the door. Do not try to move your daughter. They'll need to make sure her spine is secure before they transport her. I know you're scared. I know you're worried. I know you don't want to leave her, but the best way you can help her right now is to let the paramedics do what they're trained to do. Do you understand?"

I nodded, swallowing the lump in my throat.

"Ms. Roberts? Do you understand?"

Yes, dammit.

"Ms. Roberts?"

It took me a moment to realize. She couldn't see me nod. I croaked out an affirmative.

"Good. Would you like me to stay on the line with you until they arrive?"

The sirens grew louder. The ambulance would be here momentarily. I needed to get up, go down, meet them. The lady on the phone had said so.

I wobbled to my feet, stepped on a block, stumbled. My ankle twisted. I think. I turned towards the landing. It was only when the stairs didn't come into view I noticed I was blinded by tears. Swiping at my eyes, I walked, joltingly, one step at a time, down the stairs. The reedy voice faded. I looked down, wondering if I'd lowered the phone's volume by accident. My hand was empty.

I didn't stop. I made it to the front door, reached out, and twisted the knob. I pulled, but the door didn't open. I pulled again, harder. The door wouldn't budge. Outside, the sirens were so loud they'd become unbearable, and I could see flashes of red and blue slashing through the window blinds. I pulled again.

What the hell is wrong with this thing? Why won't it open? I was on the verge of losing control when some part of my subconscious whispered to me.

The door is locked.

I wasn't so far gone as to not feel embarrassed, but it passed with the forceful knock that came only seconds later. Flipping the bolt, I once again twisted the knob. This time, the door opened without resistance. Two paramedics rushed past me, while a third introduced himself, but his name didn't penetrate the haze that had settled over me.

I motioned vaguely toward the stairs, then woodenly followed them up. I watched as they examined Lucy, took her vitals. Next came the opening of the eyelids and the pass of a flashlight, followed closely by the careful application of a tiny neck brace. Then they splinted her arm. I heard the sickening crunch as they popped her shoulder back into its socket. She didn't budge, and I suppose I should have been grateful she was unconscious. I think I'd have preferred to hear her scream.

This time, I couldn't hold it back. I barely made it to the bathroom in time. When my stomach was finally empty and had ceased its seizing, I made my way back to the bedroom, flushed and covered in a fine sweat. They'd managed to get Lucy onto a child-sized gurney. Two lifted her and headed carefully down the stairs. The third stepped towards me, my phone in his hand.

"Ms. Roberts? Ms. Roberts."

"Mrs."

"I'm sorry?"

"It's 'Mrs.' Roberts. I'm married."

"My apologies, ma'am. We need to go. If you'll come with me?"

"My… My husband, he needs to know."

"We'll call him."

"He's at work."

"Yes, ma'am. We'll get a hold of him. C'mon, now." And taking my arm, he moved me down the stairs and out the door with a suppressed urgency. Blinding sunlight. Huge step. Hands at my waist. A boost.

"Sit here, Mrs. Roberts. Hold on."

The slam of a door. Siren screaming. A jerking lurch. Increasing speed. I stared at the opposite wall of the ambulance, purposely avoiding the flutter of activity only feet away.

It's my fault. My daughter's going to die, and it's my fault. I hadn't been there, hadn't been watching her closely enough.

What had I been doing, anyway? What was so damned important?

"... Mr. Roberts, my name is Jamey, I'm a paramedic. Your daughter has been in an accident ..."

It's my fault.

"... headed to Blessed Memorial ..."

It's my fault.

"... we're not sure yet, the doctors will have more information ..."

It's my fault! **It's my fault! IT'S MY FAULT!**

My world turned upside down. It took a moment for me to understand one of the paramedics had shoved my head down between my knees. My chest was tight, burning. I was gasping for air. Black dots were swimming in my vision. I recognized the signs.

I was having a panic attack.

"Mrs. Roberts! Mrs. Roberts, please, I need you to breathe!"

I fought it, tried to break its hold on me. It was too late; I was firmly ensnared in its clutches. Tears streamed down my face. My breath wheezed in and out of my lungs, the sound reminiscent of a drunken donkey. My arms were tight as a vice round my midsection; I was desperate to hold myself together. It wasn't working. I was falling apart, my body ripped into bloody pieces, my mind fractured into shards of hysterical glass.

"She's going to die. She's going to die. She's going to die."

"Mrs. Roberts."

"She's going to die. She's going to die."

"Mrs. Roberts."

"She's going to die."

"Mrs. Roberts!"

A set of hands shook my shoulders. My head rolled; I managed to lift it, met the eyes of the paramedic. *Jamey? Was that his name?* I was shaking violently. "She's going to die, isn't she?"

"Mrs. Roberts, we are going to do everything we absolutely can. I can promise you that. We will do everything we can. But I need you to calm down. I'm not trying to be rude here, but if we're going to help your daughter, we need to be able to focus. On her. What's her name?"

Lucy. He's right. They need to help Lucy. I finally gained control of my lungs, dragged a full breath down deep, let it release slowly.

"Mrs. Roberts?"

"Lucy. Her name's Lucy."

"Good, alright, thank you. We're almost there. And I swear to you, we're going to do everything we can for her."

I sank into a bubble, wrapping it around myself like my thick pea coat in the snow. Maybe if I held it tightly enough, I could keep reality at bay. Maybe it would all just go away. Maybe it wasn't actually happening. Maybe it was only a dream—a nightmare I would wake up from any minute. Lucy would be on her knees in my bed, shaking my shoulder, saying "Mommy, you've slept enough! Get up!" *It's all just a bad dream, right?*

The ambulance pulled up in front of Blessed Memorial Hospital's emergency entrance. Jamey placed a gentle, but restraining hand on my shoulder so the other two paramedics could rush the gurney inside. I watched my daughter, so small and fragile, disappear behind the sliding doors. My heart thudded in my chest. My breath hitched. I could feel the panic rising again. I fought desperately to control it. *Please God, don't let this be the last time I see my daughter.*

Jamey escorted me inside and led me down an aisle separating two rows of curtained-off trauma bays. Lucy was behind one of them. I tried to figure out which one, but Jamey wouldn't let me stop. We took a right, stepped through another set of double doors, and came to the admissions counter. The woman behind the desk stared at a computer, her hair swarming about her head in riotous red curls. Librarian's glasses perched on her nose. She barely glanced up as she barked, "Patient's name?"

"Roberts. Lucy."

"And you are?"

"Her mother. Susan Roberts."

"Date of birth?"

"Mine, or...?"

"The patient's."

"Oh. March. March 21, 2012."

"Address?"

There's something to be said for rote memorization. You say the same thing enough times, sooner or later you can rattle it off in your sleep. Or in an emergency room, with your child behind a curtain, alone, probably dying, while you answer tedious nothings. For a stranger, no less, either too numb or too uncaring to grace you with simple eye contact, let alone sympathy.

Unexpected fury rose in me. Suddenly, all I wanted to do was scream at this red-headed bitch who was more concerned with the information on my driver's license than my severely injured daughter. *Can't this wait? Lucy needs me. If she wakes up, and I'm not there...* The thought made my stomach churn. Once again, I fought down the rising nausea.

"Where is Lucy?"

The woman kept typing.

I looked up at Jamey, intent on asking him. He was gone. I glanced around frantically. *Where was he?* Turning, I pushed against the double doors we'd just come through. They wouldn't budge. Reaching up to my tiptoes, I peered through the small glass cutouts. There was no sign of him. Had he really just left me here? Without a word?

With no other choice, I turned back and tried again.

"Where is Lucy?"

"Ma'am, if you'll just have a seat, someone will be with you..."

"Where the hell is my daughter?!" My voice cracked, the shout bouncing off the walls and drawing the stares of everyone in the waiting room.

That got the ginger's attention. Her gaze shot to mine, her face a study in shock and newfound wariness.

"Ma'am, uh, Mrs. Roberts, please, I understand you're worried, but if you could just have a seat..."

"Damn right I'm worried, you condescending bitch! My daughter is hurt and you won't tell me where she is. That's all I want to know! Where is Lucy, where is she?!"

I was screaming now, hysterical anger taking control. Before I could stop myself, before I even realized my intention, my hands swiped across the counter, sending flyers, business cards, ink pens, and consent forms flying.

Horror at my actions was a douse of frigid water. I froze, my hands flying to my mouth. My eyes widened. My cheeks burned with mortification.

"I'm sorry." The whisper was so quiet, I barely heard it myself. I cleared my throat, tried again. "I'm sorry. I didn't mean to do that, I ... I'm sorry."

"It's alright, ma'am. Please, just have a seat."

"No, I should ... I should pick these up, I should ..." My voice trailed off, and I knelt, reaching out, attempting to put order back to the chaos I'd created.

A hand on my shoulder, along with a deep, authoritative voice, stopped me. "Mrs. Roberts?"

I glanced up, met the steady gaze of man in a white coat. "Yes?"

"Hi. I'm Dr. Whitcomb. Would you mind coming with me?" He offered a hand, helped lift me to my feet, and led me to a corner across the room where it was quieter, a bit less crowded. Then he turned to me, his expression solemn and serious.

"Mrs. Roberts, can you tell me what happened?"

"I ... I'm not sure. She was in her room playing. I was

downstairs working, and I heard a thunk. I assumed she'd just knocked into a wall or something. She does that pretty often. She's fairly clumsy, but she's always okay. When she didn't answer me right away, I got worried and went up to check on her, and I found her on the floor. She was already unconscious. I don't know if she tripped, or if she fell out of bed. I … I didn't see. I don't know. I should know. I should have been watching her, I should have been …."

The man shook his head and laid a hand on my shoulder. "No. Mrs. Roberts, please, don't do that to yourself. Accidents happen. We can't watch our children every second of every day. At some point, we have to let them test their wings. There's no way to guarantee you could have stopped what happened, even if you had been watching. The best thing we can do now is focus on doing all we can to help Lucy heal. Okay?"

I nodded. I think.

He rifled through a chart; I assumed it was my daughter's. "I've done my initial assessment. Lucy has a dislocated shoulder and a couple of broken ribs, as well as a serious head injury. She did suffer a fairly severe seizure during the initial exam. Based on that, and the suspected nature of the injury, I believe she has an intracranial hemorrhage, which means her brain is bleeding. Bleeding in the brain can cause the brain to swell, causing major damage to the brain cells, which, unfortunately, can lead to a severe decrease in brain function. I've already sent her up to radiology for a CT scan to determine the size and location of the bleed, and she will be prepped for surgery immediately after."

My heart sank, lodging itself in my gut. "She needs surgery? Are you sure?"

"I'm afraid so. And she needs it now. I'm not going to lie to you, this type of surgery is incredibly dangerous. There is no guarantee that it will be successful, and even if it is, there is still the possibility that she will suffer permanent brain damage."

"Permanent brain dam..." I couldn't wrap my mind around the concept. "How much? What kind? What do you mean by that?"

"I'm sorry, but we won't be able to determine that until after she wakes up from the procedure."

"*If* she wakes up."

"Yes. If she wakes up."

I nodded, my head bobbing up and down like my husband's Matt Forte bobble-head. My lips pursed. My eyes watered. Tightness settled into my chest, fisting my ribs and squeezing.

"O—o—okay. Okay."

"Mrs. Roberts, believe me, I am going to do everything I can to help Lucy. I can't promise you anything more than that, but I can promise you I will try like hell to bring her back to you. I need to go now, but I will have someone update you periodically, and I will come find you as soon as the surgery is over."

He placed a hand on my shoulder, gave it a light squeeze, and then he was gone. I glanced around. *What do I do now? Where do I go? Do I stay here? Where's Charlie?* I pulled out my phone, pulled up my contacts. My thumb floated over the dial button.

"Susan!"

I spun around, then raced into Charlie's arms. They came around me, so thick and strong. And suddenly it was all too much. I burst into tears, clinging to his shirt, sobs spurting from my throat. Charlie was so good. He didn't ask any questions. He didn't tell me to calm down.

He just held me. Rocked me. Whispered trivial words of comfort in my ear.

He let me fall apart. And he would be there to pick up the pieces and put them back together.

Finally, after I don't know how long, I quieted, the sobs receding into mere hitches. I drew a deep breath into my lungs and pulled back, ready to face my husband, his questions, and the inevitable, horrific possibility that we may never see our daughter again.

I summed up what happened, from the moment I heard the noise in Lucy's room, to the call with emergency services, the ambulance ride, and finally to the doctor's diagnosis.

"I'm so sorry, Charlie. I should have been watching. I should have been there. I should have—I don't know—done something. I don't know what happened, but whatever it was, I should have stopped it. I should have kept it from happening."

"Susan, Susan, stop. Don't torture yourself, please. Even if you *had* been in the same room, you may not have been able to do anything. It was an accident. Accidents happen. Lucy plays rough; she always has. And she's clumsy as hell. She can go from point A to point B without missing a step and still be covered in bruises. It's just part of who she is."

I nodded, tears welling again in my eyes.

"Shh, come here." He pulled me into his arms again.

"I was so scared you would blame me. Hell, *I* blame me."

"You shouldn't. And don't worry. She's going to be fine. She's our little wrecking ball. She'll be fine."

"I know. I know she'll be fine." I hesitated. "But, Charlie? What if she isn't?"

He didn't answer that.

I knew why. It was the same reason I hadn't allowed myself to think more than two minutes into the future. I couldn't bear to imagine a world without my daughter. He couldn't either.

After a few moments of uneasy silence, we both seemed to realize we were still standing in the middle of the ER's waiting room. We moved back to the admissions desk, Charlie's arm secure around my waist.

The redhead was gone, replaced by a young blonde who I

95

swore couldn't have been out of high school more than three days.

"Excuse me?" I leaned into Charlie, let him do the talking. Exhaustion was slowly taking hold as the adrenaline of the morning seeped away.

"Yes?" The blonde looked up, smiled. "Can I help you?"

"Yes, um, my daughter came in a while ago with a head injury. The doctor was taking her up to surgery, and I was just wondering, where should we go? I mean, where should we wait to hear how she is?"

"Oh, I'm so sorry to hear that. I hope she'll be okay. Yeah, you'll want to head to the surgical waiting room. It's up on the third floor. So take those elevators over there up to floor three, then take a right. You'll pass a nurses' station, then you'll take a left, and the waiting room will be on your left. You should be able to just follow the signs."

"Thank you. Thank you very much."

"Sure. Is there anything else I can do for you?"

"No, that's all."

"Okay. Again, I hope your daughter is alright."

"Thank you. We do, too."

And with that, Charlie and I headed toward the elevators.

The waiting room walls were a pale peach, the chairs upholstered in a light, floral pattern. Soft rock drifted quietly through camouflaged speakers. The scent of vanilla cloyed my nose in a not-so-subtle attempt to mask the distinct smell that screamed hospital. It was a room designed to be soothing, to calm frazzled nerves.

It failed. Its mishap was evident in every face that looked up as we walked in.

Full of people just like us, this room forced us to face reality. Our loved ones were in danger, and they might not make it out alive. It was a room full of ghosts: the spirits of those come before us whose futile hopes had been shattered. It was a room haunted by the echoes of *"I'm so sorry,"* and *"We did everything we could."*

I hated it instantly.

Perching on the edge of a seat, knees tight, arms resting on my legs, I bowed my head and accepted the cup of steaming coffee Charlie brought me from the machine in the far corner. Despite its warmth, I shivered. I was cold. Something sinister in the back of my mind whispered I'd be cold forever.

"It's going to be okay, Susan."

Charlie's hand found the small of my back, rubbed. I nodded. It was a platitude, and we both knew it. But what else could we do? Believing anything else seemed like a betrayal to Lucy. We couldn't give up on her. We had to believe she'd be alright.

She was always alright.

She was our Lucy.

Time passed interminably. Charlie and I didn't say much; talking took too much effort. I was using every ounce of mine just to hold myself together.

What if she dies?

Charlie said she'd be alright. But he didn't know that. What if she wasn't? What if she lost her ability to speak? What if she didn't remember who we were? What if she …died?

My mind rebelled against the thought. *No. Don't go there. Don't even think it.* But what choice did I have? I had to face reality.

The coffee churned in my stomach. The spot behind my jaws tingled. I dashed across the room, making a frantic grab for the trashcan. I barely made it.

Vomit spewed from my mouth, slapping disgustingly against the pile of discarded Styrofoam cups and napkins. The scent of stale coffee assaulted my nose, and I heaved again.

"Susan?" I heard the concern in Charlie's voice, felt his presence behind me. But my body was in the throes of being violently ill. I shook my head, then threw up some more.

Finally my stomach was empty. The dry-heaves subsided.

I was clammy, my forehead covered in a sheen of cold sweat. I rose slowly, my muscles twitching, shaky. Charlie reached out, and I latched onto his arm, accepting his assistance as he helped me back to my seat.

Embarrassed, I glanced around, wondering if anyone had noticed my ordeal. They had. Honestly, was there any missing it? Their gazes told me they were grossed out, but they got it. They understood. They forgave me for the distasteful display.

I sank back in the chair, this time with my head against Charlie's shoulder, resigned to do nothing but wait. Every little while, a man or woman in scrubs would walk in, look around, and call out a name. Every time I caught the flash of blue, I straightened, my heart speeding up in my chest. Every time someone else's name was called, the pit dropped back into my stomach.

The waiting was unbearable.

Eventually, I drifted away into that mental space between asleep and awake. It was a hazy place, where reality and dreams melded into a pseudo-truth, where everything was actually happening, even when I knew it wasn't.

"Mr. and Mrs. Roberts?"

I shot up, the blurry grogginess dissipating like fog. Charlie, too, had straightened from his slouch. We stood together, rushed over to the young female standing in the doorway.

It wasn't Dr. Whitcomb, obviously. But I didn't care. She was here about my daughter.

"Is it Lucy? Is she okay? Please, tell me she's okay." I sounded hysterical. I knew it. I couldn't stop it. "Please, what's going on with my daughter?"

"Mr. and Mrs. Roberts, I'm Dr. Miller. I'm a surgical resident, and I'm working with Dr. Whitcomb on Lucy. He asked me to come out and give you an update."

She paused then and glanced down at her hands. When she didn't go on, I prompted her.

"Well?"

She looked back up at me, at Charlie, and I could tell she was struggling. Because the update she'd brought wasn't good. My heart sank.

"Say it. Please. Just tell us."

"We've reset her shoulder, and the ribs should heal on their own. But the bleed in Lucy's brain is more severe than the CT scan initially showed, and the surgery is taking longer than expected. Dr. Whitcomb is doing everything he can to repair it, but the chances of permanent brain damage have increased significantly."

"But … she's still alive?"

"Yes, she is still alive. We're going to do everything we can to keep her that way. I need to get back now, I only have a moment, but Dr. Whitcomb wanted you to know we're still working. He'll be out to speak to you as soon as the surgery is finished."

She's still alive. That was all I heard. All that mattered. It was easy to ignore what Dr. Miller said about brain damage. This was Lucy. My wrecking ball. As long as she was alive, she could overcome anything. As long as she was alive, she'd be fine.

"Thank you, doctor."

She nodded, turned, and disappeared behind swinging doors that said *Authorized Personnel Only.* Charlie escorted me back to our chairs. I dropped into it, whispering to myself.

"She's alive. She's alive. She's alive." It was my mantra, my rope of hope, which I clung to for dear life. "She's alive. She's alive. She's alive."

Charlie took my hand, gripped it in mine. "She's going to be okay, Susan. Everything's going to be okay. I promise."

The waiting went on. The hands on the clock continued to tick, going round and round in endless circles. People came. People went. There were shouts of relief, cries of despair.

Which will we make?

My back ached from sitting in the straight-backed chair. My face was clammy. My foot had gone numb from its incessant, restless tapping. I wasn't sure how much more of this I could take. If I had to wait much longer, I was going to shred my skin!

Just when I thought I couldn't take a minute more, Dr. Whitcomb appeared in the doorway. His hair stood in haphazard tufts, as if he'd been running his fingers through it.

Stress circles lined his eyes, and his mouth was turned down in a grim frown. He looked around until his gaze found mine.

And I knew.

My arms wrapped tightly around myself. I leaned forward, shook my head. *No. Lucy was fine. She was always fine.*

Dr. Whitcomb crossed the room, squatted down in front of my chair. I heard him introduce himself to Charlie, saw them shake hands in my peripheral vision. But none of it truly registered.

Lucy's fine. She's always fine.

"Mrs. Roberts? Susan."

I forced myself to meet his eyes, still shaking my head.

"No. Don't say it. She's fine. She has to be fine."

Sympathy flooded his eyes. He reached out, took hold of my hand. "I'm so sorry, Mrs. Roberts. We were able to stop the bleed, but by the time we did, the damage was done. The bleed caused severe swelling of Lucy's brain, and there are no longer any signs of brain function. She is out of surgery, and while the machines we have her on are technically keeping her alive, Lucy is brain-dead."

"She won't wake up."

Dr. Whitcomb shook his head sadly. "She won't wake up. I'm sorry, Mr. and Mrs. Roberts. So very, very sorry."

I curled into a ball, shaking my head furiously. *No. This wasn't happening. She was fine. She would wake up and be fine. Lucy was always fine!*

I fought the sobs back, but they wouldn't be contained. They ripped free from my chest in loud, sharp bursts, drawing the eyes of everyone in the room. I didn't care.

"No. No! Lucy!" Charlie's arms came around me, hugging me close. My fingers curled into his shirt. I held on to him, this, the only point of gravity left to keep me connected to something. Anything. If I let go now, my world would spin completely out of control, and I would be launched into the nothingness of space, left to drift aimlessly forever, with no air to breathe. No life to live.

His shirt was soon soaked with my tears. But I couldn't stop. I was sure I would never be able to stop.

Eventually I realized Dr. Whitcomb was still there. I didn't know why. Then, he spoke.

"Mr. and Mrs. Roberts, I'm sorry, I know this is an extremely difficult time for you. But the fact is, you have a decision to make. Would you please both come with me?"

A decision? What did he mean? What decision?

Charlie's arms lifted me; I shuffled along beside him, letting him bear most of my weight. Putting one foot in front of the other seemed to take way too much effort. Much easier to be dragged along, following blindly, making random turns at meaningless corners.

Nothing registered.

Not until we stepped through a door. Dr. Whitcomb pulled back a curtain, and there was my daughter, so small and frail in her hospital bed, tubes sticking out of her nose and mouth, eyes shut, skin pale, head wrapped in stark, white gauze.

No. This wasn't happening to me. This wasn't my daughter. This was happening to someone else. This was someone else's daughter. For some reason, I was playing witness to another mother's agony. Because this couldn't be happening to me. God wouldn't do this to me. He wouldn't. He wouldn't let my beautiful, smart, curious, awe-inspiring daughter die.

101

She was too good. Too special. He wouldn't take her from me, He wouldn't!

But nothing could change the fact that it was Lucy in that bed. Lucy, who couldn't breathe on her own. Lucy, whose heart would stop at the flip of a switch. Lucy, who would never wake up again. Never laugh again. Never tell me another knock-knock joke. Never twirl in the tutu her grandmother had made for her fourth birthday, dreaming of being a ballerina. Never again recite her combined version of *The Billy Goats Gruff* and *The Three Little Pigs*. She would never again crawl into my lap and hug me, repeating over and over, "Hey, Mom, I love you!"

Tears streamed down my cheeks as I stared at this tiny person who was my daughter, but no longer my daughter. I couldn't change it, no matter how much my mind screamed in denial.

Lucy was gone.

And then realization hit. *A decision to make.*

"You want us to pull the plug." Dr. Whitcomb and Charlie both looked over at me as I watched Lucy. "That's the decision you said we had to make."

"I don't *want* any one course of action, Mrs. Roberts, unless it's what you and your husband want. But yes, that is the decision I was referring to. We can, of course, keep Lucy on life support. The machines will continue to breathe for her, to pump her heart, but without proper nutrition, without physical activity, without the necessary neural responses, her muscles will deteriorate, and eventually her organs will fail. Whatever decision you make, I will support it, and act accordingly."

I looked up at Charlie, desperation in my voice. "She could wake up, Charlie. She could come back to us."

His eyes brimming with tears of his own, Charlie shook his head. "She won't, Susan. You know she won't."

He was right. I knew he was right. But saying it out loud

seemed like we were giving up on her. I didn't want to give up on her. I didn't want to say goodbye. *Dammit, I'm not ready to say goodbye.*

I clung to him, fighting the tears. Failing. I felt him nod to the doctor, and my heart took up permanent residence in the pit of my stomach. It was the right thing to do. I knew it was the right thing to do. It wasn't right, wasn't fair to make her suffer, to make her hang on for me. But the thought of letting her go was like a knife in my gut.

How had this happened? How did we get here? How did we go from a perfect, normal family to … to this?

A woman brought in paperwork. Charlie signed it. The woman went away, murmuring condolences. A nurse came next. With a look of sympathy, she unhooked the tubes in Lucy, switched off the machines. Only the heart monitor was left on. Dr. Whitcomb remained, silent and unobtrusive, waiting to officially declare our daughter dead.

I clung to Charlie, weeping, telling him I was sorry. He would never be able to convince me this wasn't my fault. I had killed my daughter. I hadn't been paying attention, hadn't been doing my job as a parent. I had failed as a mother. I'd left her alone, left her unattended, too concerned with myself, my work. I hadn't been there for my child, and now she was dead.

The beeping slowed, stuttered. And then all that was left was a high-pitched drone. That horrible, high-pitched drone. It went on and on, until Dr. Whitcomb stepped forward, reached up, and hit a button. The sound ceased, leaving only the harsh breaths coming from Charlie's and my lungs. Dr. Whitcomb unwound his stethoscope from his neck, leaned over, and placed it against Lucy's small, and unmoving, chest. He rose back up, glanced at the clock on the wall.

"Time of death, 16:47. Mr. and Mrs. Roberts, I'm very sorry for your loss."

She was gone.

I pulled away from Charlie's embrace, stumbled over to the hospital bed. Pulling Lucy's body into my arms, I held her. Rocked her. And sobbed.

"I'm sorry, Lucy. I'm so, so sorry! Oh, God, I'm sorry, I'm sorry, I'm sorry!"

I don't know how long I sat there before Charlie came over, disentangled Lucy from my arms, and pulled me into his.

"We need to go, Susan."

"I can't leave her, Charlie. I can't ..."

My head spun, and everything went black.

When I woke up, I was in a hospital bed. There was an IV in my left arm. A nurse was standing near, scribbling in a chart.

"Wh ... what happened?"

The nurse looked up. "Oh, you're awake! How are you feeling?"

I felt out of it. What had happened? The last thing I remembered was holding Lucy. She was... I didn't want to even think the word. Had it really happened? Or had it all been a horrible dream? *Please, God, let it have been a horrible dream.*

"My daughter. Is she okay?"

"Oh, the baby's fine. The doctor says you passed out from dehydration and stress. But you're going to be fine. Some fluids and observation, and we should be able to get you out of here. As for the daughter part, well, it's too early to tell. Are you hoping for a girl?"

I stared at her in confusion. A sinking sensation danced in my gut. "What are you talking about? Where's my daughter? Where's Lucy?"

The nurse mirrored my confusion. Her mouth opened and shut, like a goldfish searching for its last meal. Just then, Charlie walked in. One look at his face, and I knew it hadn't been a dream. Tears immediately filled my eyes.

"She's really gone, isn't she?"

Charlie just nodded, came over to sit next to me, and gathered me into his arms. "Yes, Susan. She's gone. They just took her down to the morgue."

The nurse was watching us, a dawning horror crossing her features. She flipped through the chart, read, then hurriedly grabbed her things and rushed towards the door.

"Wait!"

She hesitated, then turned back at my call.

"You asked … You asked if I was hoping for a girl …"

She looked at me as if I were at once judge, jury, and executioner, and she'd just been condemned. She glanced toward the door, searching for someone to pardon her. No one came.

"I'm sorry, I just started my shift, I didn't know … I didn't realize, about … I … I thought you knew."

"Knew what, exactly?"

"You're six weeks pregnant."

PHOBIA

September 2, 2015

Reyna slouched in the overly padded couch, her arms tucked tightly against her chest. She stared determinedly out the slanted blinds of the window, blatantly ignoring the rest of the room, and the woman who sat across the way, watching her.

The woman's gaze was as heavy as a ton of bricks. Still, Reyna didn't look away from the window. She had no intention of meeting Dr. Mannolo's eyes.

"Reyna?"

She didn't answer. Just flexed her arms and squeezed harder.

"Reyna, I understand how you're feeling."

Bullshit.

"I can help you, if you'll let me."

Reyna's lip quirked up in a cynical sneer. They all thought it was so easy to understand, so easy to diagnose, so easy to *do something* about. They had no idea.

"Reyna, you do understand being here is a prerequisite to you keeping your job, right?"

She shifted, swallowed, pursed her lips.

"And that doesn't mean just *being* here. You have to participate. You have to try. You have to talk to me."

I don't have to do a damn thing. You can't make me.

"Reyna, do you want to keep your job?"

Honestly?

"Well, it's your hour." Reyna heard a creak. "We can spend it however you like."

Reyna peeked out of the corner of her eye. Dr. Mannolo had leaned back in her chair, with her hands folded on her stomach. She was still watching Reyna, but there was a hint of resignation tinging her patient attitude.

Reyna shrugged, resettled herself deeper into the couch cushions. She didn't want to talk. She wasn't going to talk. She'd find another job, where different coworkers knew nothing about her. She'd control herself better. Avoid the triggers. No one would need to know, and she wouldn't have to talk about it.

A weighty silence fell, broken only by the monotonous tick tock of the dour, circular clock hanging above Dr. Mannolo's head. Reyna glanced at it. 10:18. Eighteen minutes. Only forty-two left to go.

It was going to be a long hour.

October 14, 2015

"When did you have your first panic attack?"

Reyna glanced at Dr. Mannolo, then away. The blinds were fully open today, allowing the dreary light of the overcast day to filter in. It was a perfect setting in which to discuss the events that had started her slow, swirling descent into mental decay. She might have smirked at the cliché, except the last time she'd checked, her anxiety provided no source of amusement; she certainly wasn't laughing.

"I was twelve."

"Twelve?"

"Yes."

"That's young."

"Gee. I'm sorry I didn't tell the damn thing it was early and to come knocking in another year or two."

"I didn't mean it that way, Reyna. It wasn't a criticism, merely a comment."

Reyna squirmed, glanced back outside. Raindrops were

trickling down the glass now, in a myriad of twining trails. "I know. I'm sorry."

"You have nothing to apologize for. It's part of the disorder, Reyna, and that's not your fault."

Except it sure felt like her fault. If she could control herself better, if she could just talk herself out of the impending attacks. They didn't have to happen. She could stop them, if she really tried hard enough. And each time she didn't, she failed. Again and again, she failed.

"I was in my martial arts class. We were working on defense that day, ways to break holds, get away from an attacker. I was the oldest, so I went last. When Sensei Foster called me up, I expected him to grab a fist of my hair, like he had with the younger girls. That's what I was prepared for. But he didn't grab my hair."

She trailed off, remembering the day in perfect clarity. The familiar claws of panic teased the edges of her mind. Her skin prickled. To ward it off, she wrapped her arms around herself, stood, and walked over to the window. If she'd known then. If she'd known then that was the beginning, and it would lead to this …

"What did he do?"

Tears pricked her eyes. Swallowing hard, she let the memory wash over her.

"He tackled me to the ground. He straddled me. Then he grabbed my wrists and pulled them above my head. At first, I didn't think anything of it. I knew how to get out of this hold. All I had to do was buck my hips and throw him off balance. And I did it. But …"

"But what?"

"He didn't let go. I bucked again, harder. And again. I yanked my wrists, trying to break his hold. But he wouldn't let go. I kept trying the same maneuver, over and over, thinking sooner or later he would acknowledge that I was doing the technique correctly. He would ease his grip and let me go.

But he didn't. No matter how hard I tried, he didn't."

The first tear plunged down her cheek and splashed to the floor. She swallowed and continued.

"I think then, subconsciously, I understood what he was doing, the situation he was trying to enact. I developed young, and I didn't look twelve. I looked, well, older than twelve. But I was still too young to understand that put me in a lot of danger from unwanted attention. Until that day. All of a sudden, he wasn't my Sensei anymore. I didn't know who he was. All I knew was that I had to get away. Somehow, I had to get away from him. That's when I really started to struggle. And scream. I screamed at him for not letting me go. At the other students for not helping. At the parents sitting on benches just beyond, watching but not intervening. Even mine. I screamed, and fought, and kicked, and bit. The adrenaline rushed in, and I finally managed to roll him off me. And then I lost it. I hit him as hard as I could, over and over and over again. And then I ran."

"Where did you go?"

"To the bathroom. I locked myself in a stall, curled into a ball on the floor, and cried. I couldn't breathe. I couldn't think straight. I was so scared whoever that person had been was going to follow me in here and attack me again. That's when I had my first panic attack."

Reyna fell silent, watching the coming storm. Her tears dripped in tandem with the raindrops on the window.

"I'm sorry that happened to you, Reyna."

Reyna shook her head and wiped her eyes. With a shrug, she turned and plopped back on the couch. "Whatever. Turned out to be a good thing, as it so happens."

"And why's that?"

"Because it wasn't a full year later before some teenage asshole tried to rape me in the showers at the public pool. That training session was the only thing that kept me from losing my virginity at thirteen."

Dr. Mannolo's eyes widened, presumably because of Reyna's bluntness. Reyna didn't care. Her foot twitched to an unheard and incessant beat. She drew her brows down, hooding her eyes. Folding her arms across her chest, she stared at the floor and released an impatient huff, slamming the door on the subject.

"So, are we done for the day, doc? I don't want to talk about this anymore."

October 31, 2015

Reyna leaned against the wall, arms crossed, eyebrows drawn and lips pursed, glaring at the sea of undulating bodies, and inwardly cringing at the obscene number of fake cobwebs dangling from the walls. *Dammit.* She never should have let Stacy talk her into coming to this stupid thing. Stacy was currently the life of the party, dancing it up in the middle of the floor, her pelvis permanently glued to some dude dressed like Elvis. She'd abandoned Reyna about forty-five minutes ago.

Why am I still here? She'd asked herself that half a dozen times in the last hour. *Why'd I even come in the first place?* Because much as she hated to admit it, some of the garbage Dr. Mannolo said was getting through to her. She couldn't avoid her triggers forever, and crowded places were definitely one of them.

So when Stacy knocked on her door with the flyer about the campus-wide Halloween party, Reyna grudgingly agreed to go. *Big mistake.* Now she was stuck here, in a slutty, gothic vampire getup, no less—*What the fuck is wrong with me?*—watching her best friend act like a tramp.

Her mood darkened from slate to obsidian. She could have been snuggled in bed, with a bag of Reese's and a Michael Myers marathon. But no. She'd listened to her crack of a psychiatrist and instead of a relaxing and solitary All Hallow's Eve, she was fighting her fears and hating every damn second of it.

"Fuck this." Pushing herself away from the wall, she headed for the door. She'd call a cab. Hell, she'd walk if she

had to. Either way, she was so done with this shit. She was nearly to the door when something heavy barreled into her.

"Hey, watch it, jackass!" Her shoulder blazed with pain, and she whipped around to confront whatever asshole had just slammed into her.

"Holy sh — I'm so sorry. I wasn't paying attention. Are you okay?"

"I'll live." Reyna glared at a pair of wide shoulders. She glanced up, only to suck in her breath at a pair of blood red eyes.

"Don't freak. They're contacts, I swear. The only concession I'd make in coming to this thing. I'm, Kyle, by the way."

"Reyna."

"Reyna … Hey, don't you have Chem 2 with Renauldi on Tuesdays and Thursdays, ten am?"

"So what if I do?"

"Nothing. It's just, I have it, too, and I thought you looked familiar."

"Must be the teeth." She flashed the fangs she purchased earlier that day — *How the hell did Stacy talk me into wasting twenty-five bucks on these things?* — and turned back toward the door.

"Hey, wait!"

Reyna stopped, glanced over her shoulder, a single eyebrow raised.

"Do you wanna dance?"

November 4, 2015

"Why didn't you dance with him, Reyna?"

Standing back at the window and staring out, Reyna shrugged. The day was clear. The sun was bright, but not enough to keep the autumn chill away. Red and yellow leaves crackled underfoot and blanketed the quad. Normally, it would have been her favorite kind of day.

"Reyna?"

"I don't know."

"Reyna." The tone of censure grated, like the squeal of tires after a gunshot. She cringed and curled her shoulders forward.

"Did you *want* to dance with him?"

I did. I still do. Which is precisely why I didn't. She dipped her head in the barest of nods.

"So, why didn't you?"

Because I'm scared. Because the last three guys I've gotten involved with wigged out when I inevitably had an attack. Because people look at me differently and think there's something wrong with me. Because it's easier to be alone.

"Reyna, I keep telling you. At some point, you have to open up to people. And I don't mean me; I mean others, too — friends, family, and yes, occasionally strangers. You can't keep all this fear pent up inside you. At some point, you have to take a chance on life."

What she said made sense. The words were in the right order. They were logical. Probably even right. But Reyna couldn't help but mentally rebel at them.

She wanted to get better. She did. That's why she kept coming to these godforsaken appointments. Every Wednesday, rain or shine, she showed up at Dr. Mannolo's office. She walked through the door, sat, listened. Sometimes, she talked.

She *wanted* to try. She just wasn't quite ready. It was like staring at a roller coaster for the first time. It was alluring; it drew you in and tempted you to get on. But those six or seven loops that sent the world spinning … For just a little bit, you couldn't help but hesitate.

She couldn't help but hesitate.

A rough exhale of breath drew Reyna's gaze. Dr. Manno-lo was watching her, exasperation and sympathy warring on her features. Kinky curls cloaked round cheeks and chocolate eyes, and her usually plump lips were pulled into a thin, tight line.

"I'm sorry, Reyna, but the hour's up for today. I'll see you next week."

Reyna nodded and headed for the door, attributing the pit in her stomach to the tarantula decals leftover from the Halloween festivities still clinging to it. Except she knew better. For the first time, she got the feeling Dr. Mannolo was truly disappointed in her. She shouldn't have cared. But she did.

December 18, 2015

Reyna sat in the back of the class, staring at, but not registering a word of Professor Renauldi's final exam on quantum theory. She was too busy glancing up at the back of Kyle Turner's head. His hair was black—like, Dave Navarro, jet black—and it looked so damn smooth and silky. She wanted to run her fingers through it, let the softness spill over her skin—

"Ms. Fuller?"

Reyna jerked from her musings and glanced guiltily at Renauldi. "I'm sorry?"

"It must be difficult trying to read with your chin."

"Oh, I'm sorry, Professor. It won't happen again."

"Let's hope not. Your grade cannot afford to suffer anymore, Ms. Fuller."

Reyna blushed at the whispered inference of her less than ideal grades, and refocused on her test. Out of the corner of her eye, she caught Kyle's gaze. He gave her a quick wink, then turned back to the front. Reyna allowed herself a tiny smile before trying her damndest to pay attention.

When the bell finally sounded, Reyna gathered her things slowly, packing them away in her bag with excessive attention. Carrying her test to the front, she handed it to Renauldi, not daring to meet his gaze. Once the paper was out of her hands, she made a beeline for the door.

Kyle was waiting for her just outside.

She couldn't pretend to not see him. So, with a deep breath, she approached him.

"Hey, Kyle."

"Hey, Reyna."

She glanced at the floor and shuffled her feet. "I ... well ... How'd you do on the test?"

"Okay, I think. How 'bout you?"

She shrugged. "I have a feeling, not so hot."

"Well, don't worry about it now. No point in letting it spoil the holidays, right? I mean, c'mon. It's only quantum theory. Nobody gives a shit about it, except crazies like us."

"I guess that's true. Well, I should probably get going. I've got one more final before I'm done, and I—"

"Do you want to go out with me?"

"What? You mean like on a ... a ..."

"A date, yes."

No. I should say no. Nothing good can come from dating him. I know that. He's too good-looking, too well-known. He's popular, for fuck's sake, at a massive campus where the concept of popularity has no business existing. Besides, I'm due for an attack any day now. It's been too long. Hell, it's been, what? Six months? I can't avoid it, and what's a guy like Kyle going to do when I collapse into a ball of frayed nerves for absolutely no fucking reason? He'll do what every other guy has done: look at me like I'm nuts and move along to the next girl in line.

Except ...

This is what Dr. Mannolo is talking about. Letting people in.

114

Giving them a chance. I don't know how he'll react, and that's IF I have an attack. Maybe I won't. Maybe he'll never know. But am I really going to live the rest of my life shutting people out because they might walk away someday? Besides, I want to say yes, dammit.

It was easier, that was for sure. But standing here, staring up into Kyle's peridot eyes—so much better than the red contacts—she wasn't sure she wanted easy anymore. Before she'd made a conscious decision, she heard herself speak.

"Yeah. Yeah, a date sounds good."

January 27, 2016

"So how are things going?"

"They're good. Surprisingly so."

"Oh? And why is that?"

Because Kyle's different from any guy I've ever met, and he doesn't seem to care that I'm a nutcase. Because I'm happy for the

first time in I can't remember how long, and I'd forgotten what happy feels like.

"Reyna? Why does it surprise you that things should be going well?"

"Things don't go well for me, doc. I've been a slave to my mental state for too long."

"Except you're not a slave to it—"

"Yeah, I know. I know you say I can control it. But when I'm in the middle of an attack, it doesn't feel like I can control it. And when I'm constantly on edge, waiting for one to rear its ugly head, I don't feel in control."

"That's because you have to *take* control."

"Easier said than done."

"I know that."

"Do you? I wonder sometimes."

Dr. Mannolo sighed, folding her hands in her lap. "Reyna, I handle cases like yours all the time. I deal with the entire anxiety spectrum, from chronic worry before a test to agoraphobia. I've been researching anxiety for twenty years now, and I can tell you, your panic attacks are something you can conquer, because they're nothing more than illusions."

"What, you're saying they're not real? That I make them up?"

"No, that's not what I mean at all. All I'm saying is that, while they may manifest themselves in physical symptoms — the shortness of breath, the pounding heart, the cold sweat — they are actually occurring in your mind. With some mental exercises, you can learn to control them, and ultimately, keep them from happening. You can learn to control your breathing, you can force your heart to slow. You can stop the panic from dragging you under."

"It sounds simple, Doc. But it's not. Not when you feel like you're going to die."

"But you're not going to die, Reyna. These attacks can't kill you. You know that, right?"

Reyna nodded and released a pent-up sigh, letting her head droop. She did know it; she just wasn't sure she believed it.

"So, you said things are going well. Care to elaborate?"

Reyna found herself smiling in spite of herself. *Kyle.* Kyle was all the elaboration needed. They'd been dating for nearly two months now. The time had flown by; even now she still couldn't believe he was still dating her. *Except I haven't had an attack in front of him yet, have I?*

"Stop. That thought you just had, Reyna. It was negative. It shows on your face. What was it? Can you tell me?"

Reyna sighed, then dove in. "Things with Kyle are going well. He's just such a great guy. I mean, he's sweet and romantic, but he's not overbearing. He has a, let's call it unique, sense of humor, and he has this sixth sense about what he can and can't appropriately joke about with me. He knows when to talk and when to listen, and he doesn't care if I just want to be quiet. He just … gets it. Gets *me*."

"So what's the problem?"

"I … I haven't had … an attack in front of him yet."

"Okay. And?"

"Well, it's going to happen eventually. And then this will all be over. And I'll be left standing here with a broken heart."

"Why?"

"What do you mean 'why?'"

"Do you know you're going to have a panic attack?"

"Well, no, not for sure, but—"

"And why would a panic attack, if you indeed have one, mean that things will end between you two?"

"Because guys don't stick around with girls like me."

"You mean girls with anxiety issues."

"Yes."

"Reyna, I'm not sure you're giving this man nearly enough credit. Have you tried talking to him about your anxiety?"

"Hell no."

"Why?"

"Because things are going well, and I really like him, and call me crazy—because I am—but I want to spend as much time with him as I can before he realizes I'm a freak."

"Reyna, you're not a freak. You're living with clinical anxiety that's linked to a set of certain phobias: claustrophobia and arachnophobia. Thousands of people suffer from them, as well as hundreds of other phobias, each one irrational. And many, just like you, suffer from panic attacks when faced with the triggers of their phobias. It's a fairly common condition, and it doesn't mean there's anything wrong with you. It's not something that should cause you shame. If you get anything out of these sessions with me, Reyna, let it be that. You have nothing to be ashamed of."

She knew that, too. Convincing herself of it, however, was another matter.

"Can I ask you something, Reyna? Something extremely

117

personal?"

"Sure."

"Have you been physically intimate with Kyle?"

Reyna's gaze shot up at Dr. Mannolo, and her cheeks reddened. She glanced away before answering. "Yes."

"More than once?"

"Yes."

"Regularly?"

Reyna nodded.

"So, if you can share that part of yourself with him, if you can trust your body with him, why not this?"

Reyna opened her mouth, but nothing came out. Clapping her mouth shut, she came to a realization; she didn't have a good answer.

June 18, 2016

"I think you're enjoying this just a little too much."

Kyle grinned at Reyna's words as he cinched the restraints holding her wrists a bit tighter. She winced as the leather lightly pinched her skin, and fidgeted, trying to ease the sensation. Feeling the tug and knowing what it meant, she shivered as anticipation, tinged with anxiety, scuttled down her spine.

"I think you're right."

He glanced up at her before sliding down the bed to adjust the ties around her ankles. With a final tug, he sat back on his knees and gazed down at her, his eyes ripe with satisfaction. Naked on the bed, she lay spread eagle, wrists and ankles trussed to the thick bedposts. Kyle's eyes raked over her body, pausing to linger on her breasts and then moving lower to stare at her core, wide open and exposed.

Reyna shivered beneath his scrutiny, nerves and anticipation warring within her. She still couldn't believe she'd said yes to this. But then again, things with Kyle had progressed with nary a hiccup, and despite her lack of sexual exploits—and her fear of being trapped—this felt utterly natural. The last six months had been a godsend: no attacks, no major anxiety, not even the slightest stirring of panic. She'd nearly quit going to see Dr. Mannolo, mostly because the woman wouldn't stop harping on her about telling Kyle about her disorder. *Why?* Reyna wanted to know. They weren't bothering her anymore, so why bother?

And Kyle. Kyle was absolutely perfect. Six months in, and she was head over heels in love. The good news was he seemed to be as crazy about her as she was about him. She'd met his parents and introduced him to hers. Just last week he'd asked if she would consider moving in with him.

Everything happened so smoothly with Kyle. Why, in the past she never would have considered giving up her control, especially in a sexual situation; what little control she felt she had over her life she kept well in hand. But this? This felt ... right. It was bold; it was exciting. It was the type of challenge Dr. Mannolo would usually encourage her to embrace. *Wouldn't she be proud, if she could see me now? Not just wading into the pool of bondage, but jumping in headfirst.*

The thought had her hesitating. *C'mon, now. Don't start. This doesn't really count as BDSM, anyway. They're just restraints. It's not like he's planning on whipping me with chains. Still ...*

"You're sure about this, Kyle?"

"Nothing bad is going to happen, baby. You're completely safe. Trust me."

It was weird, because it was unusual—and completely unexpected—but she did trust him. And maybe—and that was a big one, of course—if she could do this, maybe she *could* tell Kyle. But she'd think about that later. Right now, she was going to relax. And enjoy.

Her skin tingled, the first stirrings of arousal burgeoning as Kyle leaned down to nip at her left ankle. He moved upward, leaving a trail of chaste kisses along her calf. Pausing to linger at her knee, he ran the tip of his tongue along the groove that led to the back of her leg. Then he worked his way higher, running his mouth along her inner thigh, inching closer and closer still to her core. A mere whisper from his destination, he stopped and then followed the same path up her other leg.

Coming once again to the juncture between her legs, he released a warm exhale of breath that teased and tickled her clit. She moaned. Her eyes fluttered shut, her hips lifting instinctively off the bed. Kyle chuckled, then slid up her body, the skin-on-skin contact just enough to drive her crazy. He settled in beside her. Breath held, she waited. Nothing happened. After a moment, she opened her eyes and turned her head to find him staring down at her, an amused smile on his lips.

She pouted. "You're teasing me."

"That's half the fun."

"Maybe for you." She shifted restlessly. She was spread wide, stretched open. She had no way to release the pleasantly painful pressure steadily building between her legs. She was completely at his mercy, subject to his will.

What did I get myself into?

He laughed, then lowered his mouth to hers. She opened for him; his tongue delved down to dance with hers. His hand, warm on her skin, settled on her hip, then slowly slid up to cup her breast. His thumb lightly caressed her nipple, bringing it to peak before moving to wake up its twin. Soon after, his mouth followed in his hand's wake. The wet heat of his tongue drove her wild. She squirmed beneath his attentions, twisting and writhing, fighting against her bonds. Her fingers curled, grasping for something, anything. She wanted to touch him, to tease him, to torment him as he was tormenting her.

His hands and mouth roved over her, creating an ebb and flow of yearning as he brought her to the edge of fulfillment and then pulled back. Again and again she neared the brink, fighting desperately for release. Again and again he denied her, keeping her firmly in a state of frenzied need, a state of pleasure that bordered on pain.

Her moans grew louder and wilder, the tugs on her restraints harder, more insistent, as she begged him to let her orgasm. His breath turned harsh, and she grinned. He wouldn't hold out much longer. In a few moments, he'd thrust into her, hard and fast. Her hips lifted in invitation. He cursed, and she released a pent-up laugh. *Finally* ...

And then he was gone.

A sudden chill prickled over her damp skin as his body heat retreated. *What the hell?* Her eyes flew open and shot around the room frantically. Kyle was up and off the bed, standing close to the door panting, eyes hot, cock erect and straining. He watched her for a moment, a smug and satisfied smile on his lips, then turned to leave. Her expletive brought him back.

"What the fuck, Kyle?"

He chuckled. "What?"

"Don't you 'what' me. Where the hell do you think you're going?"

"To take a shower."

"Excuse me?"

"To take a shower," he repeated.

"Why?"

He shrugged. "To get off."

"Isn't that what I'm for?"

"Absolutely."

"So, you're going to let me up?"

"Nope."

Wherever he was going with this, she wasn't getting it. The incessant pulsing between her legs screamed for attention, her body demanding release; her mind could process nothing else.

"What is going on, Kyle?"

"You said I could do whatever I wanted to you, remember? Whenever I wanted. So, I'm going to go jack off in the shower, and then I'm going to come back, and we'll start all

over. I want to see how long you can stand it. I want you dying for me before it's over."

He winked. With a laugh, he left the room, leaving the door only slightly cracked. Down the hall, the bathroom door clicked shut, followed by the dim sound of the shower. Moments later, the indistinct thumping of drums joined the distant mix; he'd flipped on the radio.

"Kyle? Kyle!"

Incredulity and fury bubbled within her. Was he actually serious? The asshole was just going to leave her here, all hot and bothered, while he gave himself a hand job? Reyna thrashed in earnest, yanking at her bonds, trying to get free. But the harder she pulled, the tighter the restraints held. After a few minutes, she flopped back on the bed, resigning herself to the fact that she was good and caught. Her frustration spun inward as she realized while that knowledge irked, it also aroused. She was as turned on now as she had been five minutes ago when Kyle was all over her.

Huffing in irritation, she settled in to wait. With nothing better to do, she studied Kyle's room. She'd been in it before, but she'd never really taken the time to look around. The two of them were usually more concerned with getting into bed. Next to the bed was a nightstand, Kyle's reading glasses, and a copy of *1984* tossed aside. On the far wall was a dresser; one of the drawers was ajar, a white wife beater peeking out. On his desk was a laptop, covered in tattoo shop stickers, and above was a New York Giants poster. She still didn't get that. They lived in St. Louis. But then again, the Rams were headed to L.A.

Finally, she glanced up at the ceiling. Her eyes caught and she froze, the fire of her arousal immediately doused by a chute of icy terror. The first pricks of panic skittered along her skin as she stared, paralyzed, at the arachnid a mere six feet above her head.

"K-k—Kyle?" Her voice squeaked out, weak to her own ears. The sounds of the shower and the radio still poured from the other room. And wait … *Is he grunting? Asshole.* The thought fled as she glanced up again at the wolf spider clinging to the top of the wall.

It shuffled, moving an inch or two down the wall.

"Kyle!" Her voice grew stronger. "KYLE!"

The din of the water continued. The music played on. There was no click of a doorknob. She looked up again and, knowing it was useless but unable to help herself, tugged roughly at the restraints.

The damn thing was huge, at least three inches long. It moved again, scuttling another few inches down the wall, and for a split second the scene froze, and she could sense everything in perfect clarity.

She could make out the individual hairs on the spider's body and legs. She could count its eight individual eyes; staring up in horror at it, she was sure she recognized some level of intelligence. The fucker was staring right back! The sounds coming from the bathroom sharpened; she recognized Blue Oyster Cult's "Don't Fear the Reaper." The light scent of imminent sex mingled with the spicy notes of Kyle's cologne and rose up to tickle her nostrils. A slight soreness was developing in her muscles from undulating as she'd chased release, and the chafing around her wrists and ankles burned. Her throat was slightly raw from panting.

The spider moved again, and the moment shattered. Terror set in, enslaving her.

Her muscles tensed. Her chest constricted. Beads of a cold sweat bubbled up from her skin and popped, leaving her chilled. Breath released on a whoosh—Had she been holding it?—then stuttered back in with a gulp. Recognizing the beginning signs, Reyna desperately fought to hold off the impending attack. But the panic ignored her, its sharp hooks burrowing deeply into her flesh.

Dr. Mannolo's image drifted in her head, reminding Reyna to take deep breaths, to remain calm. *The physical symptoms are real, but the panic is just an illusion. This isn't real. The fear isn't debilitating. The panic doesn't have to dominate you. You, Reyna, are in control. Not the panic. You.*

But the harsh, rapid sawing of her breath drowned out her psychiatrist's voice. Her muscles spasmed, trembling violently. Her skin froze under a coat of gooseflesh. She opened her mouth to scream, but her throat locked. An invisible hand pressed on her airway, cutting off her ability to inhale. Her mouth gaped open and close, like a fish out of water, begging for breath and finding none. *You're full of shit, Dr. Mannolo! If this isn't real, why I can't I scream? Dammit, let me scream! Kyle!*

Plastered to it, her eyes followed the eight-legged creature as it made its way down the wall, its hair-covered legs lithe and pliant, carrying its body in a smooth and easy glide. Someone else—a biologist, maybe—might have appreciated the steady grace of its movements; she only knew the stretch of empty wall between her and it was rapidly shrinking.

Her heartbeat spluttered, then raced. It jumped in her chest, playing its own mocking version of paddleball, bruising her ribs. In response to the abuse, her ribs shrank in on themselves, a python's coils around her lungs, limiting her access to oxygen. Her vision wavered, a hazy grey overtaking the edges of her sight until all she could see was the wolf spider, growing ever larger, looming ever closer, until finally it reached her.

Stretching out a single long leg, the spider found her forehead and braced, then reached out with another and fully planted itself. Each leg singularly brushed her skin in quick succession as the spider dropped from its perch on the wall and glided down her cheek.

Holy shit, get off me! Please, God, get it off me!

The spider slid down her neck, following the trail Kyle's lips had taken so recently. Shock mingled with disgust as she responded. Already highly sensitized, her nerves fired with arousal at each stroke of the spider's legs. Its movements seemed deliberate, each of its eight legs specifically placed to rouse and incite, almost as though it not only sensed her response, but encouraged it.

Reaching her shoulder, the wolf spider made its way steadily across her collarbone, then down her sternum toward her breasts. Her heart pounded. Her lungs heaved, but she couldn't move; terror kept her immobilized. Looking down at herself, she watched the massive arachnid making its way along her body. Much as she wanted to, she couldn't pry her gaze away.

Horror washed over her as it mounted the rise of her breast. Reaching the border of her rosy areola, it hesitated, considering, then stretched out a single front leg, and brushed it lightly against Reyna's nipple. Immediately, her nipple hardened. Hot wetness seeped between her legs. The response stunned her into motion. She thrashed wildly, trying to dislodge the thing from her body. Refusing to be moved, the spider merely moved to cover her nipple with its body, crouching low over the peaked tip, the hairs on its abdomen brushing against her.

Tears flooded her eyes, streaming down her face as helplessness swamped her. Rational thought fled, giving way to the horror, as her body betrayed her, succumbing to arousal caused by something she hated and feared.

The racing of her heart, propelled by panic, was a cruel mockery of the pounding she'd felt when Kyle had teased her with his hands and mouth. Her pants were now gulps of terror instead of gasps of pleasure. Muscles were tense now with cold terror, rather than warm anticipation. And still the arousal lingered, her body hungering for release.

It should have been funny.

Why is my body doing this? Am I really that desperate for release? And why can't I fight the panic? Dr. Mannolo had asked her, more than once, how long would it take her to learn to control her fears. She'd pushed Reyna to try, urged her to conquer her disorder. *Why the hell didn't I try harder? Why didn't I listen?* Now Reyna lay there trembling, unable to resist as the spider continued to make its way down her body. Her skin continued to tingle, disgust warring with stimulation. Her mind rebelled, yet her body yielded.

This can't be happening. Please, God, don't let this happen!

Reaching her navel, the wolf spider took a moment to explore the small dip in the flat plain of her stomach, then moved lower. Reaching out with its legs, it stroked the lips of her labia. The first rumblings of release threatened. She fought against it, trying desperately to hold out. *I don't want it now. Please, stop! I don't want this!* Then the spider found her clit. Stroking it first — once, twice — it moved. Sliding its hairy body across her fully, it settled onto her, applying pressure. Claiming her.

Reyna exploded, the wave of the orgasm drowning her in a mixture of terrified pain and tumultuous pleasure. That's when she broke. All control lost, the panic finally trapped her in its dominating clutches. Her hold on reality dissipated.

In that moment, Reyna left her body. Floating along the ceiling, she looked down at herself, tied to a bed, naked and helpless. *What in heaven or on earth possessed me?*

Though her mind had disconnected, her body lingered in the agonizing throes of the lingering orgasm and the uncontrollable panic attack. Unable to blink, her torrid eyes itched. She couldn't inhale. Her raw throat bore the bruises of forcing air from already empty lungs. Her heart pulsated, galloping under her skin, desperate to break free of its cage. Her chest cramped, strangling her, as the spider finally left her vulva and made its deliberate way down her shaking leg. Every muscle she possessed tensed, straining to break free from both the physical bonds of the restraints and the mental lock of the panic.

As the wolf spider strolled down the length of her bare skin, Reyna understood her situation was dire. Her heart rate speedily increased, flying at a rate it could not healthily maintain. Her lungs screamed for air but were denied. Black spots dotted her vision as her brain began to shut down from lack of blood and oxygen. *No! I don't want to die! I can't die! Dr. Mannolo, you said panic attacks can't kill me. You said! They can't kill me!*

She watched as the spider danced along her toes, then finally left her skin, crawling onto the mattress, and disappearing down the side of the bed. She might have breathed a sigh of relief but for the panic that had taken hold and refused to let go, dragging her down into a quicksand mire of hysterical terror.

Suddenly, there was a slight change in her pulse. She shouldn't have felt it; maybe she didn't. Though it should have been impossible, her heart raced even faster, followed by a slight fluttering, an irregular quiver that provided an awkward counter rhythm to the breakneck pounding.

It was almost musical. It was …

ABOUT THE AUTHOR

Briana Robertson excels at taking the natural darkness of reality and bringing it to life on the page. Heavily influenced by her personal experience with depression, anxiety, and the chronic pain of fibromyalgia, Robertson's dark fiction delves into the emotional and psychological experiences of characters in whom readers will recognize themselves. Her stories horrify while also tugging at heartstrings, muddying the lines of black and white, and staining the genre in multiple shades of grey.

In 2016, Robertson joined the ranks of Stitched Smile Publications. Her solo anthology, *Reaper*, which explores the concept of death being both inevitable and non-discriminatory, debuted in 2017. She also has stories included in *Unleashing the Voices Within* by Stitched Smile Publications, *Man Behind the Mask* by David Owain Hughes, Jonathan Ondrashek, and Veronica Smith, and *Collected Easter Horror Shorts* and *Collected Halloween Horror Shorts* by Kevin Kennedy.

She is currently serving as Head of Dark Persuasions, the dark erotica branch of Stitched Smile Publications.

Robertson is the wife of one, mother of four, and unashamed lover of all things feline. She currently resides on the Illinois side of the Mississippi River, with a backyard view of the Saint Louis skyline, and is a member of the Saint Louis Writers Guild.

FIND OUT MORE

Author Website: www.brianarobertsonwri.wix.com/brianarobertson

Facebook: www.facebook.com/brianarobertsonwrites

Twitter: @Briana_R_Author

Instagram: @wyfnmmarbrtsn

Email: brianarobertsonwrites@gmail.com

ALSO BY BRIANA ROBERTSON

Baby Grand

ANTHOLOGIES
(Including stories by Briana Robertson)

Collected Halloween Horror Shorts
Collected Easter Horror Shorts
Man Behind the Mask
Unleashing the Voices Within